Jenna C
Mysteries

VOLUME ONE

AIRSHIP 27 PRODUCTIONS

Published by Airship 27 Productions
www.airship27.com
www.airship27hangar.com

Editor: Ron Fortier
Associate Editor: Gordon Dymowski
Marketing and Promotions Manager: Michael Vance
Production designer: Rob Davis

ISBN: 978-1-946183-91-0

10 9 8 7 6 5 4 3 2 1

Jenna Coyne Mysteries

VOLUME ONE

By Robert Ricci

Contents

Blood on the Cobblestones

Jenna Coyne glanced up at the travel information board at North Station, as she had done for the previous four months, wide eyed and a little apprehensive. It wasn't that the trains ran on an erratic schedule or anything. In fact, it was just the opposite. The Haverhill train departed at ten minutes past eight every morning, and for the most part, on the same track. Still, Jenna was weary of that first time being late for work.

She had just graduated last May, and after a few false leads, discovered that her parents nagging suspicions about the false value of her college degree were proving to be hauntingly correct. They had prompted her to seek out a career in the medical or science field, but stubborn Jenna had decided to major in Arts, with a specialty in modern literature. As her parents predicted, finding employment had been a tiresome chore.

Her luck had changed half a year ago, when by chance, she landed a job in an insurance agent's office. Well, it wasn't actually by chance. A friend of her mother's had given her a glowing reference and Mr. Esposito had hired her immediately. Thus began her daily ritual of watching the large overhead screen at North Station which touted hourly train arrivals and departures.

Her nervousness was caused by her employer's punctual obsession. William Esposito insisted she be at her seat and ready to answer calls at exactly 9am. Time is money was his motto. Only problem is, he didn't seem to be making all that much of it. In fact, the phone never rang more than half dozen times a day.

So far, this hadn't proven to be a problem for Jenna. He had agreed to pay her 38k a year to start, with a promise of possible commission. While this wouldn't offer her a lavish lifestyle, it was enough to rent a one bedroom studio in Boston's historic North End, and for that Jenna congratulated herself on her progress.

There was just one interesting problem. William Esposito liked to stare at her. Not all day, and not at all times, but enough to give her pause and question his intent. He was twice her age and married, yet the vibe he gave off was unmistakable.

Her reverie was interrupted by a blaring voice over the loud speaker informing that her train was ready for boarding. As she did every day, for five days a week, Jenna Coyne grabbed her portfolio by the shoulder strap and headed out onto the platform to begin her travel.

A creature of habit, Jenna sat in the third car, third row on the right. Most of the passengers around her had the same intentions, so the cast usually echoed the previous days' ensemble, usually, but not today. Today would be different.

Jenna smelled him before he actually sat down. The odor of stale beer was undeniable. It made her nose twitch, and she instinctively pushed up her glass frames. She tried to appear nonchalant as she twisted slightly in her seat to catch a glimpse of the passenger who had taken up residence in the seat behind her.

What she saw did not come as a surprise. The man was about forty years old, with long scraggly hair and a face that could stop traffic. His eyes met hers and he greeted her with a gap mouthed smile that revealed a serious need for dental reconstruction. He winked once, raised a brown bag, which she ventured contained his morning pick me up, and settled back in his seat with his feet up on the chair.

Jenna was taken by surprise. Junkies and drunkies usually rode the MBTA, not the more expensive commuter rail. The fact that she paid close to three hundred dollars a month to ride this train seemed like an insult when someone of his ilk could board and ride. She felt a sudden twinge of guilt and prejudice for thinking that way, so she turned and settled into her seat.

The ride seemed ordinary and non- eventful right after that. The conductor had come by and collected fares, and apparently her grimy friend had enough money to purchase a round trip ticket to Malden. She would have to put up with the stench until then. For now she would just sit back and read a dog eared Piers Anthony Xanth paperback that she had picked up for a dollar at the Brattle.

It was a muggy June day, and she had dressed accordingly in a plain white blouse and tan skirt. Her hair had been tied up with elastic to keep the sweat off her neck, and fortunately the train's air conditioning unit was working gloriously. After fifteen minutes or so, she allowed herself the luxury of closing her eyes and resting her head against the vinyl seat in an attempt to meditate before subjecting herself to another boring day at Esposito's insurance agency.

Her daydreaming didn't last long. She felt the tug on her golden tresses and her mind snapped back to reality. She turned around and glared at the dentally challenged passenger behind her.

"Keep your damn hands to yourself creep!"

Only she didn't utter those words. Instead a slight murmur escaped her lips and caused her tormentor to giggle.

"My bad," he snapped. "I thought a bee was on your head."

Jenna had no verbal response but instead rolled her eyes and turned her back on him hoping the incident was over.

No such luck.

"Is this your real hair color? " Crooked Teeth asked. "Or did you get it from a bottle?"

Jenna looked around. There were about twenty other passengers traveling in her car, yet none of them made eye contact with her. She tried to mentally will them to gaze her way.

"Leave me alone!" she whispered. "I'm going to call the police."

Crooked Teeth looked hurt, and then a smile broke out on his face. He resembled a demented version of Tim Curry as the Grinch. Without warning, his hand shot out and a greasy palm landed on her shoulder.

"Please, I just got out of Nashua Street, and I can't go back there. I meant no harm."

Jenna's skin trembled under his touch, as she pulled back from his grasp.

"I'm calling the conductor."

Crooked Teeth said nothing to counter her threat. He slowly sat back in his chair and stared out at the scenery as the train shot past some of the colorful landmarks.

"Sorry." He croaked. "But you're so beautiful"

That was the last straw for Jenna. She snatched up her portfolio and stood up ready to leave her seat. What happened next she found unfathomable. Crooked Teeth also rose and placed his hands on her hips.

"Marry me?"

Jenna shimmied out of his grasp and hurried down the aisle to the next car. To her dismay, not one person offered assistance or even appeared to have witnessed the assault. She didn't look back until her eyes narrowed on a conductor and she was able to get his attention. Within seconds her story was told and a promise of justice was made.

Justice wasn't as swift as Jenna had hoped. Crooked Teeth was apprehended at the next stop, but Jenna also was detained to fill out a transit police report and make a commitment to file charges. This resulted in her being an hour and a half late for work.

Of course, she had called William Esposito, or Bill as he preferred and he appeared sincere in his concern and horror when told of the incident. When she finally got to the office, he told her to forget about the phones today and just sit back and catch her breath. He whipped her up a fresh cup of coffee from the office Keurig and hung her portfolio on the coat rack.

She smiled at him with genuine warmth, feeling a little guilty about her morning assessment of the little man. True, he tended to leer at her and his vanity was overwhelming. Despite being over fifty years of age, Bill Esposito fancied himself a player. He dyed his hair jet black, and tended to dress like a character from a seventies movie. It didn't help his cause that he was slightly over five feet tall and sporting an obvious toupee. Still, he had given her a chance when other doors had been shut, and for that she was grateful.

"It must have been awful?" He offered. His outfit today consisted of polyester grey slacks and a button down mauve colored shirt open to the chest revealing a few gold chains.

Jenna nodded and sipped at the beverage. Her nerves were finally calming down when the ringing of the phone startled her. Instinctively, she reached out for the receiver, but Esposito beat her to the handle.

"No, no. Let me pick it up. It's probably my wife reminding me to stop for bread or something." He smiled, revealing perfect teeth, the result of years of dental upgrades.

Jenna smiled and tried to ignore the chatter of the phone conversation. It was indeed Mrs. Esposito on the line. Jenna had never met her, but the woman seemed pleasant enough when she had called the office.

"Got it. Take care." Bill mumbled into the phone while writing notes on the pad at the reception desk. He turned to Jenna. "She called to remind me to pick-up my dry cleaning."

"I could go get it." Jenna announced.

Esposito shook his head vehemently and dragged over the rolling chair.

"You will do no such thing." He waved his hand over the chair. "Today's assignment is to rest."

Jenna arched an eyebrow.

"What about time is money?" She begged.

Esposito feigned a heart attack.

"You pain me young woman. You are an investment. Without you I'd be swamped with work and God forbid Mrs. Esposito leave the gym or beauty parlor to lend a hand."

Jenna giggled and took another sip of the coffee.

"Ok, Mr. Esposito but only for a few minutes," she stated.

"Nonsense my dear. You sit down right now and close your eyes."

Jenna did as instructed. She removed her glasses and allowed herself to slink back into the leather chair. She sighed and closed her eyes.

"That's more like it. Be comfortable. Kick off those shoes," he suggested. "I'm declaring this an office holiday."

Jenna bobbed her head in acknowledgement and slid off her pair of Dr. Scholl's. Her eyes remained shut and she placed the coffee down securely on the desk.

"Thank you Mr. Esposito" she whispered.

"Please, it's been four months. I think it's ok to call me Bill."

She snorted. "Bill, I could get used to this."

The words were hardly out of her mouth when she regretted saying them. She tried to backtrack. "What I meant was..."

"Shhh." He silenced her. He had stepped behind her chair and she could smell the faint touch of his cologne. It was very appealing.

That was when William Esposito made his move. It wasn't an abrupt attack or anything, but a subtle introduction to his true motives.

"You're so tense." He commanded. "Let me massage your shoulders."

Jenna felt an odd sensation as his fingers gripped her lightly around the neck and collarbone. His touch was warm and inviting, and she felt oddly perverse at the hint of enjoyment she displayed when a slight moan escaped her lips.

"Feels good huh?" his voice was soothing and she felt his breath on her neck as he whispered it into her ear. Still, she didn't open her eyes.

"It does." She gasped, the tension easing out of her body with each caress. She was in heaven, and then he had to go and ruin it.

"I'd like to feel good too," he suggested placing her hand in his. Her eyes opened widely, but he persisted. "Maybe we can help each other."

She tried to resist his grip but his strength was deceptive. He drew her palm to his crotch, and placed it there firmly. She could feel his throbbing manhood, threatening to burst right through the thin material.

"What are you doing?" she yelped, revulsion in her voice.

"Please Jenna, I'm lonely." He was stroking his erection against the fabric of his trousers. "My wife and I, we ..."

Jenna wasn't interested. She bolted from the chair and pulled her portfolio down from the coat rack with such force that the entire rack upended.

She stared at Bill Esposito in disbelief.

"I can pay you?" Was all he could mutter in defense.

Jenna shook her head. Forgetting her glasses she headed toward the door. Her only thought.

"How could this day get any worse?"

The trip home was uneventful. The commuter train had arrived on schedule, and before she knew it Jenna was headed down Commercial Street on her way to her modest studio. The air still stifled her breath from the mugginess, and even though she couldn't wait to get home, her daily ritual of stopping at the corner convenient store hypnotized her until, without knowing it, she was inside the White Hen Pantry.

She welcomed the rush of cool air venting from the air conditioner.

"Hello Gina!" a cigarette tinged voice greeted her. It was Mr. Maxwell, the owner of a little plant shop over in the Financial District.

"Hi, Grant. How's business?" She managed as politely as possible.

His intuition immediately caught her tone of desperation.

"I can't complain, but looks like this weather has got the best of you."

Jenna released an exaggerated sigh. "Day from Hell." She responded. "I just want to get home and forget everything."

Grant Maxwell let out a belly roar. "You're just getting your feet wet. Take it easy, and things will work out," he paused. "Drop by my shop this weekend and pick something out. On the house, of course."

Jenna flashed a huge grin. This gentle old man had restored her faith in humanity. "It's a deal, but only if you let me bring you a cannoli from Modern."

"It's a date, but don't tell my doctor." He shouted, walking away.

She proceeded to purchase some milk and two bottles of Mountain Dew Code Red, a vice she couldn't quite quit and secretly didn't want to.

Within minutes, she had turned at St. Leonard's and made her way to the entrance of her outdated apartment directly above a print shop. That fact had given her worries when she first moved in, but she found the walls were almost soundproof and the noise never made its way up to the second floor.

She lived in 2A, an old brownstone that required the gas stove to be lit with a long match, as well as an equally appealing circular bath tub that somehow managed to keep the water in despite the 360 degree turn of the shower curtain.

Jenna immediately opened the kitchen window to allow the stale air to escape. She then turned on the bath tub faucet to let the rusty water run for a minute until it became clear enough for her to feel safe.

She removed her glasses and stared at herself in the mirror. Sweat dripped from her forehead, and her tongue was dry from lack of moisture. She released the elastic from her hair, and shook out the golden strands. After a moment she concluded verbally. "Not bad for someone who was almost molested today."

Her dad told her she looked like Marisa Mell, a minor actress from the late sixties to early seventies. Jenna had googled her image, and although she was pleased for the comparison to such a beautiful woman, it creeped her out a little that it had come from her father.

While the water ran, she listened to her voice mails. The first was from William Esposito as she had expected. She listened half-heartedly as he repeated the word sorry about two dozen times. The second message was from her best friend and former college roommate, Marta.

"Hey girl, me and Edna are going out for drinks at the Hong Kong tonight. Why don't you come on down and join us?"

Marta had roomed with her during her junior year at Stonehill, and the two had become lifelong friends. The Edna that Marta referred to was actually the girl's mother, a time traveling flower child who dressed in neon spandex and was only fifteen years older than her daughter. The two were often mistaken for sisters much to Marta's dismay.

Jenna had no intention of making the short journey to Faneuil Hall tonight. Even though she had decided work was out of the question for tomorrow, her weary body and aching brain made the choice to just curl up and watch a marathon of Netflix episodes.

She returned to the bathroom and promptly shut the faucet off. She squirted a few drops of bath oil into the water and started to unbutton her blouse. That was the last thing she remembered as a blunt object struck the back of her skull sending her into oblivion.

Jenna awoke to a pounding headache. She tried to inhale fresh air, and a sudden dread overwhelmed her. Her mouth had been duck taped shut. She looked down at her body. She was tied to a kitchen chair at the legs and hands. Her blouse had been removed, leaving her bra exposed. She spun her head around frantically in an attempt to assess the situation.

She was in an apartment very much like her own. She suspected it was one of the other units in her building. Her gaze drifted to the doorway, and then her heart froze. A young black man faced her, his gaze penetrating to her spine. He wore a long baseball jersey adorned with the Pittsburgh Pirates logo and a pair of baggy Adidas shorts that hung a full three inches below his boxer shorts.

"Bout time you woke. I thought Rashad bashed your brains in."

The lump on the back of her head was golf ball sized. She tried to speak.

"Don't waste your time. Shad went to get your man so we can settle this once and for all."

Jenna had no idea what he was talking about. Snots were hanging from her nostrils as she fought to breathe the acrid air.

Her tormentor smelled of body odor mixed with a metallic smell, the uncompromised greeting of a drug user.

"Sorry 'bout your top girl. I ain't like one of those guys that sticks it in any hole. I just want my money. "

His voice sounded sincere, yet his eyes danced all over her chest. She felt her fingers begin to tremble.

The door opened and another young black male stepped through. He didn't wear a Pirates shirt, nor any shirt for that matter, just a long pair of denim shorts cut well below his knees.

"Derek, tie this fool up with his bitch and see if he'll sing."

Rashad pushed a tall, gaunt red head into the room. His face was beyond pale, the only color coming from a mouse under his left eye. Jenna wondered why he didn't run, and then she saw the flash of metal the thug named Rashad had pressed to the skinny boy's back.

"It doesn't have to be like this," the ashen faced boy said, his words deliberate and slow.

Derek moved across the room with lightning speed and punched the white boy hard in the gut. The kid buckled to one knee, a hand before his face.

"Shut your damn mouth or I'll slice your skank from ear to ear. " Rashad mumbled. "You brought this on yourself Kyle. "

Kyle dropped to both knees. His once white t-shirt now drenched in his own blood from the beating he had received. "I was gonna pay you. "

This statement seemed to infuriate Rashad more. His leg lashed out, a sneaker catching Kyle square in the nose, causing even more crimson to stain his shirt.

"Oh you gonna pay. All of it. We trusted you man. And this is how you treat us?"

Kyle began to sob.

"I worked hard for you. I made you a lotta cash," he bellowed.

"And that why you still alive." Derek responded matter-of-factly. "Truth is you are a good earner but you owe four thousand large and..."

Kyle cut him off. "Two thousand!"

Derek grabbed the pale youth by his red hair and pulled him back to his feet. "No, you borrowed two grand, so now you gotta pay back double." He wound up as if to strike him again, but instead just shook his head. "Kyle, this is a business. Everyone knows us, and if we don't act it will be a sign of weakness, so I gotta ask you to make amends. "

Kyle nodded aggressively. "Whatever you need. Maybe we can make a trade?"

Rashad had been silent during this time. His gaze had never left Jenna's frame. She feared these men would take her against her will. He came closer. Like his partner in crime, he too reeked of body odor as well as cigarettes. His breath was rancid as he dropped to all fours to face her.

"In the old days, guys would just cut off a few fingers to send the message, but I don't want to cut your digits off Kyle." He turned to face the youth. "You know why? I think you're still valuable to us, so I'm gonna give you an option."

A glimmer of hope surfaced on Kyle's face. "Whatever you need" he echoed his previous rant.

Rashad stood up and called Derek over to his side. They conferred for a minute or so in quiet whispers, until finally Rashad turned back to Kyle with an ultimatum.

"We checked around and word on the street is you love this girl more than anything. That being the case, here is my offer. You make the choice. Derek cuts off two of your fingers or we run a train on your bitch while you watch."

Jenna felt numb upon hearing this vicious tirade. She started to rock the chair and struggle against her restraints like a crazy woman.

Derek found this amusing. "I think she can't wait. I bet this whore likes taking it in the seat." He brushed a hand against her shoulder and snapped a bra strap. "Is that true Vicky, you prefer anal?"

Jenna stopped her frantic rocking. "Vicky?" she wondered. And then it hit her. Her eyes rocketed over to the youth Kyle. The swollen eye and blood had negated her perception earlier. Now she studied him intently. It came to her in a flash. "2B."

Kyle was the quiet kid who lived across the hall from her. In the few months she lived here they had exchanged greetings fewer than a handful of times, but it was the name Vicky that had triggered her memory. The youth never seemed to leave his apartment, and she had just assumed he worked from home or was a government funded freeloader. It didn't matter to her as long as he remained quiet and minded his business, but the girlfriend, she was a whole different zebra.

Vicky was a plump, short legged girl, perpetually dressed in black stretch pants that came to visit the young man on weekends. Jenna knew this because the dwarf girl usually announced her arrival in the form of a torturous ritual every Friday that consisted of her dragging a rolling suitcase up the stairwell while coughing the entire time. Jenna had opened the door a couple of times to serve notice that the racket was making noise, but the ignorant girl had never acknowledged her.

Her wandering mind drifted back to the immediate situation.

Kyle staggered to his feet. He lifted his shirt to his face and wiped a stream of blood. There was a new swagger in his step.

"Take her. Do what you want and we'll be square,"

Derek's hand shot across his face with a resounding slap.

"We won't be even until you pay the four grand. Next Friday, Kyle, or we do more than screw this bitch."

Kyle nodded his consent and began for the door. Rashad blocked his passage.

"Not so fast. You gotta watch," he paused; a thought dawned across his brow. "Even better, you gotta film us with my cell."

Jenna began rocking again. This time she tipped her chair over and the tape tore from her left wrist. She reached for her mouth but her hand was numb and the fingers brushed against it in vain. She saw Derek coming toward her again, and she tugged at the tape a second time. This time it tore free. She let out a blood curdling scream.

"You gonna be fun!" he confirmed. He dropped his Pirates shirt to the ground. "I'm going first, Shad. Give this punk your cell."

Rashad reached into his back pocket with glee, and then a strange thing happened. There was a hollow noise and then he toppled over, his eyes rolling back into his head. Before Derek could react a blue and gold blur emerged from the doorway and sprayed a substance into his eyes. Derek immediately clawed at his face, but then the same hollow noise echoed again and he went down like a candlepin.

Everything had happened so fast that Jenna could feel herself lifting from her body and then she realized that she was about to feint. As she slumbered off to dream world she heard a triumphant shout.

"Pendeho!"

This time Jenna woke to find herself in a hospital room. Her vision was blurry but she recognized Marta Ruiz.

"Oh thank God!" her friend exclaimed. Tears streaked down her face. "What was going on back there, Jennie?"

"You tell me," Jenna responded in a monotone voice. "How did I get to a hospital?"

Marta grabbed her hand and squeezed. "Mami and I saw your door open and then when you screamed she ran and got your bat and just went to town on those guys. Oh Jennie, what have you gotten mixed up in now?"

Jenna ignored the implication of that question. "Where's Edna now?"

"She saw you stirring and went to get that sergeant they sent over. "

Right on cue, Edna Ruiz entered thru the hospital room doorway. She wore shiny blue lycra pants with a knee length yellow cotton shirt emblazoned with large blue polka dots. That explained the blur that Jenna likened to a second rate Image Comics hero.

"Girl, you gave me heart failure!" Edna bellowed. "I didn't know what to think, but when I heard you scream I knew something was going down. "

Jenna began to tear up. She could sense the genuine affection these two ladies emanated toward her. "You saved my life."

Edna was about to agree, when a loud cough echoed from behind her. It came from Martin Conrad, BPD Sergeant. "She certainly did," he stated.

Marta rose from her chair, yanking at the hem of her blouse like she was back in the principal's office. "Jennie, this is Sergeant Conrad. They sent him after we filed a report while you were admitted into the ER."

Sergeant Conrad took out a small notebook. "Are you up for a few questions Jenna?"

Jenna nodded and began to tell her tale, at least as much of it as she could remember. Martin Conrad's expression never changed. He jotted notes dutifully, occasionally repeating a question, and always showing patience for her to finish speaking. When he had completed his inquiry, he handed her his business card and requested she come down to area A-1 tomorrow to sort through photos in hopes of identifying Rashad and Derek.

After he left, Marta returned from the nurse's station with the news that Jenna could leave. They all agreed that going back to the North End was not an option. Fortunately the Ruiz lived on the other side of the Callahan tunnel in the enchanted neighborhood of East Boston or as the natives insultingly referred to it as Latin America.

Marta and Edna Ruiz resided in a cozy two bedroom condo in the Jefferies Point section of Eastie. In a shrewd move, a dozen years back, Edna had gambled her life savings by purchasing it for about seventy grand. The investment had proven to be successful. The property was easily worth five times that amount now. Jenna was proud of her friend's young mother who bore a strong resemblance to actress Michelle Rodriquez. Edna Ruiz had given birth at fifteen years of age in a section of the city that was overwhelmed with young, unwed Spanish mothers. Rather than slide into the role society projected for her, she finished high school, got a job at a prestigious hotel in Copley Square, and had managed to nickel and dime her budget until she was able to plunk the down payment on her home. She was truly an achiever of the American dream.

"Thank you so much for letting me stay here," Jenna said, emerging from the bathroom. She had taken a shower and was wearing an old grey sweat suit Marta had loaned her.

Edna tossed her head back and laughed. " Please, how many times did you take care of my baby at college?"

The trio were munching on popcorn and playing the board game Trouble.

"C'mon mama, I never did anything wrong! " Marta blurted out.

Edna exaggerated her nod. "Of course not sweetie, cause Jenna was keeping an eye on you." She pressed the bubble containing the dye. It came up on three. "Madre de dios! I have no luck." She moved her piece on the board. "I was so afraid you would get knocked up like I did."

"Stop it mama. With all your preaching I'll never lose my virginity."

"Good. And always remember what I told you." She paused. "Boys just want to get into your panties. "

Marta snorted. "Nice advice Mom. Half the time you don't wear any!"

"I just tell you that so you won't wonder where I left them," she fired back.

Marta giggled and planted a kiss on her mother's cheek. "I love you, loca."

"I love you too baby."

Jenna smiled triumphantly. The day from Hell was over, and she couldn't think of a place she'd rather be than with these two good friends. "I love both of you," she whispered but not loud enough to sever the mother-daughter connection. She popped the bubble. "Six. I'm on the board."

Two hours later she was sound asleep on the sofa.

The next morning Marta dropped her off at the police station adjacent to WHDH television where she was greeted by Martin Conrad. The Sergeant was a big man, well over six feet tall and with the bulk to match. His stern demeanor was offset by the faint freckles adorning his face. Jenna reiterated her statement from last night and began pouring over the mug shots in search of her attackers.

The burly officer made small talk while she flipped through the pages, constantly reassuring her that a return visit from the pair was highly unlikely. He did recommend her landlord change the lock. While they were chatting her phone rang. It was Bill Esposito again.

Jenna listened politely as her employer resumed his apology from the night before.

"I decided we both could use some time off," he mentioned. She could imagine the sweat pouring down his face. "I'm going to take the wife to the Cape for a few days, and I think you should treat yourself to something too. How about a week's paid vacation? And we can talk about a pay increase when you get back."

Jenna hesitated and then responded, "We'll talk next week."

"Do you need me to speak to your boss? " Martin Conrad offered.

"Thanks anyway," Jenna answered. "It's a long story."

The Sergeant threw his empty coffee cup away. "You could use a break. How about we take a walk down to Mike's Pastry and you can throw together a bag of clothes while I check your place out?"

Jenna brightened at the idea, and then she remembered she was wearing Marta's ratty old sweats. " I'm a mess."

Martin Conrad smiled. His profession wouldn't allow him to comment publicly but deep inside he begged to tell her he felt otherwise.

«—»

Jenna filled a Nike gym bag with clothes and hygiene essentials while Marty Conrad changed out her door lock. They had stopped at True Value hardware as Jenna decided not to wait for her landlord to take care of it. She was packing her toothbrush when she noticed a slip of paper on the floor. She didn't recall it previously being there. Her obsessive nature would never have tolerated it. She unfurled the note and read it.

ZDV14K

A license plate? The scrawl was childish and in pencil. It had to have been dropped by one of her attackers or Kyle.

Her gaze wandered to the tub which still contained the water from her aborted shower. A tremor shot down her spine as visions of Kyle's bloody shirt swept over her.

"Just another minute," Conrad called out.

His voice snapped her back to reality. Without a moment's hesitation, she dipped the paper into the cold bath water and then balled it up. She proceeded to drop it into the toilet and then closed her eyes. She willed her mind to record the number, and then flushed the toilet.

She started to turn and smacked right into Martin Conrad. He caught her by the elbow before she toppled over from dizziness. His touch was warm and inviting.

"Sorry, my wits are still out of sync." She muttered.

He didn't release his hold until she was upright again. His eyes locked in on her. "Everything ok?" He asked. His tone was neutral, yet it still managed to extract a tinge of guilt from her. "Your door is ready," he said changing the subject.

Jenna turned to the sink and washed her hands, eager to withdraw from him. She spied the sergeant from the mirror as he reached down and unplugged the bath tub cork.

"Thanks Marty," she managed. He had asked her to drop the formality when they were parading down Salem Street. "How about we just skip that coffee and go back to the station?"

Martin Conrad didn't answer her right away. He ran his hands under the water at her sink, and then toweled them off with slow deliberation. "No, I think you've had enough for one day Jenna. Why don't I just drive you back to East Boston?"

Jenna flashed a smile of relief. "I'd like that."

«—»

Jenna napped the rest of the afternoon, her slumber constantly interrupted by the strains of mariachi music echoing from nearby Piers Park. The few times she did drift off into slumberland resulted in nightmares featuring Rashad and Derek. They reminded her of the old rap duos she liked to watch on MTV after middle school got out each day.

At last her boredom was broken by the sound of a key turning in the door. She glanced at the clock on the wall. It was a replica of one of those old fashioned cat clocks from the fifties with the big shifty eyes that clicked with each turn. Four p.m. That would be Edna, home from her shift at the Sheraton.

Edna entered in her concierge uniform, a complete transformation from the way Jenna usually saw her. She was one hundred percent business, and Jenna could focus on why this woman had risen so prominently in her position. Edna use to kid that she had blown all of upper management, but beneath her wacky exterior was a cunning and talented professional.

Jenna's admiration was immediately erased by Edna's first words upon entry. "What bitch? No margarita waiting for me?" She threw down her purse. "If you're gonna stay here, you gotta get with the program." She soldiered into the kitchen. "Magic bullet, ice cubes, tequila and margarita mix," she rattled off. "Stay with me, there's gonna be a quiz."

"Sorry Edna. I was catching up on some rest. "

"Good. I hope you got enough of it cuz it's Friday and we are going to the Hong Kong!" She blended the ingredients and poured the resulting mixture into two plastic Solo cups. "Cheers bitch!"

Jenna nursed her drink while Edna trotted off to the bedroom to get dolled up for the night out. Marta worked at City Hall, so she would just meet them there.

"Did you talk to that hunk?" Edna blurted out.

"Who?" Jenna replied.

Edna came storming out of the bedroom wearing only pantyhose and a bra. Her body was magnificent, only marred by a tiny scar on her inner thigh, where long ago, a heroin fueled admirer had mistaken her for a Thanksgiving turkey. "You know good and plenty I'm talking about the sergeant." She undid her bra and let it drop to the floor. Her breasts still defied gravity at thirty-six years of age. "He's a much better catch than that chocolate thunder gang I had to rescue you from."

Jenna was stunned. "Edna, you don't think I knew those guys do you?"

Edna paused. "Honey, I'm not judging but I did hear those posers say that white dude was your man." She peeled off her pantyhose. Jenna

Edna entered in her concierge uniform…

noticed that her friend's mom preferred to be clean shaven. "Well?"

"It's not like that. They thought I was Vicky."

"Who's Vicky?" Edna howled as she disappeared back into her bedroom. She reappeared seconds later carrying a white terrycloth tube top and a pair of powder pink leggings. She neatly folded them over a kitchen chair before stepping into the bathroom for a shower.

"My neighbor's girlfriend. That's who they were after."Jenna answered. She could hear the water running, and her mind drifted back to the license plate number. "I'm going to give Marta a quick call."

Marta worked in the Traffic Department at City Hall. She had access to the state RMV records. Jenna hesitated, not sure if she was doing the right thing. She was about to hang up when Marta answered the line. Jenna explained what she was seeking, and after a few moments of hemming and hawing, Marta agreed to research the plate. Jenna listened to muzak while she waited for Marta to return to the line.

Edna emerged from the shower, her body glistening and smelling nicely of baby powder.

"Madre de dios girl. You been home all day and you aint ready?" She dabbed at herself with the towel before hurling it onto the kitchen table. "We are going to be late and I don't like Marta being there by herself." She grabbed her sparse outfit from the chair and wrestled into it.

"C'mon, I left the mat down for you." She snatched the receiver from Jenna's hands and placed it back on the telephone stand. "Move, andale!"

Jenna headed to the bathroom only to be stopped by Edna. "Now what?" She asked jokingly.

Edna kissed her on the forehead. "Everything's gonna be alright."

Jenna had donned a more modest attire than her companion. She chose jeans and a top she had scooped up during half price day at Macy's. The ensemble was completed with a pair of flip flops which many bars and clubs denied entrance for. The Hong Kong was more casual than most of the Faneuil Hall scene. Its crowd was a blended mixture of young and old of all races and preferences. More importantly, it was cheap, and on Jenna's tight budget that fact held powerful sway.

It was still early when they arrived, the second floor not yet open and the bottom floor filled with a handful of early bird adventurers and the after work down one and go crowd. The few guys that were there instantly turned their attention to the enchanting Edna. She was the living embodiment of a Bill Ward cartoon pinup.

"There's my angel!" she squealed, spotting Marta in a corner near the entrance.

Marta was sipping from a bottle of beer which neither lady recognized. Probably from the potluck tub. The Hong Kong ran a promotion where you randomly selected a bottle of beer from a bright red bucket and it costs only two bucks. Marta, not being a big drinker, frequently chose this path to imbibe.

"For God's sake, mom! You look like you're getting ready to work the corner!"

Edna Ruiz laughed and hugged her baby girl. "Be nice baby or I'll start showing pictures of you in pigtails and braces."

"Don't you dare!"

Jenna returned from the bar with one of the restaurant's signature scorpion bowls and three straws. "Drink up Ruiz family."

Edna inhaled a large gulpful. "God that's good." She smiled at one of the doormen who had allowed his gaze to linger a little more than was considered polite. "You know they use to put prizes in these bowls, but people choked on them!"

Jenna giggled, taking in the familiar surroundings. During her sophomore year at Stonehill, they had run a pub crawl in downtown Boston and her and roommate Marta had partaken in a little too much revelry and ended up christening the bus simultaneously on the way home. For the rest of the year they had earned the title of Pukie Twins, a tale which had managed to escape Edna's notorious snooping right up until graduation day when some of the classmates disclosed the embarrassment.

The trio was more than halfway through the bowl when the karaoke began. Edna swallowed hard, and waved her hands frantically. "You two are singing tonight. I'm going to sign you up now." She shimmied off toward the bandstand giving Jenna the opportunity to interrogate Marta.

"Did you get that information?" she demanded.

"Shhh." Marta forced a finger to her lips. "There might be workers here tonight. You know I work in a den of cutthroats and backstabbers."

Better than creepy old men! Jenna thought.

Marta was also dressed in jeans, part of the city's casual dress code on Fridays. She had thrown on a silver glittering top before heading over to the pub. This was as close as she could match her mother's outrageous wardrobe. "You were right. It's a license plate."

"And? " Jenna couldn't mask her impatience.

Marta pulled out a sheet of handwritten notes. She hadn't dared use the printer for this task. "It is registered to John Robinson, 29 Elm Street in Salem."

The name meant nothing to Jenna. She grasped the sheet and put it in her purse as Edna slinked back to the table.

"We're doing Girls Just Wanna Have fun!"

Marta grimaced. "Ma! Always that Cyndi Lauper crap. It's played out just like your fashion style."

Jenna posed a large frown. "Leave my hero alone." She winked at Edna. "You look fabulous. "

Edna feigned an uppity pose. "I know." They all chortled with her, the alcohol starting to kick in. "Time for a cigarette."

Marta protested. "Mami! I thought you quit?"

Withdrawing a pack of Winstons from her handbag, Edna nodded in agreement. "I did, tomorrow." She got up and moved toward the exit, her hips swinging, commanding attention. Many a pair of eyes took the bait.

"I'll go keep an eye on her," Jenna said. "Order some chicken teriyaki. I have a feeling we might be here for awhile."

Outside, Edna had attracted a throng of gentlemen all eager to light her cigarette. Jenna stared in appreciation. Her friend truly was stunning, sleazy outfit aside. She grabbed Edna from the wolves and headed away from the pub to a quieter environment near the Custom House.

"How come you never got married? " Jenna questioned.

Edna was taken by surprise from the bluntness of the question. "Baby, that blow on the head really woke you up huh?" She inhaled a long drag of the smoke. "There have been men," she paused. "Too many men."

Jenna blushed. "No one special?"

Edna reflected for a moment and then tossed her cigarette to the ground. "No one worth losing my Marta over." She draped an arm around Jenna. There was a slight sheen from her perspiration, but she still smelled pleasant. "I didn't want to be one of those girls you see up and down Border street. You know the ones. They sit outside on the stoop all night, chatting with the men while their kids roam the sidewalks shoeless in diapers." She kissed Jenna on the forehead. "My mom was one of them. She spent her life waiting and listening to those lowlife men tell her how they were going to rescue her and take her away from the projects." A single tear rolled down her face.

"You don't have to explain." Jenna began.

Edna shook her head violently. "Let me finish. You see I was the little girl running up and down. My mother would keep me up with her so I wouldn't wake her in the morning and then one morning she didn't wake."

Jenna was startled. Marta had never spoken of her grandparents or any other family members. "What happened?"

Edna took a moment to form her words. "I was only six so I don't remember clearly. All I can recall is mama laying on the sofa with her eyes open and her friend Omar shaking her arm and yelling at her to wake up." Her lips trembled. "Because he was hungry and he wanted pancakes. Only mama didn't wake that day and Omar didn't stick around for the ambulance or the police. After that I was with a lot of different folks that day and I didn't understand much, but I remember overhearing them say she had overdosed."

Jenna began to weep. Her own thoughts drifted toward her mother, who was alive and in good health. "I'm so sorry."

Edna nodded and straightened her back. "Frustrating as this was, I started to lead the exact same life as my mother, in and out of foster homes and falling for every boy's spell until I got duped into having Marta. It was only then that I vowed never to make her repeat the life my mother and I had led."

"You turned out to be a damn fine woman." Jenna tried to lighten the mood. "Even if you do dress like a hoochie mama!" Laughter erupted from Edna. "Well hurry up before that girl turns me into a damn liar."

They were heading back to the Hong Kong when Jenna spotted an unnerving sight at the entrance to Aquarium Station. It was Vicky, the girlfriend of battered Kyle.

Edna noticed the cause of Jenna's stoppage. "You know her?"

"Yeah, yeah. An old friend. Why don't you go check on Marta while I run over to say hello."

The diminutive girl was dressed in her usual frumpy outfit of a t-shirt and black leggings. She made eye contact with Jenna but said nothing. She just sat up against the wall, motionless and cross-legged. There was an empty styro-foam cup in front of her.

"Spare some change?" Her voice was harsh and older than her years suggested. She still had not looked up.

"Vicky?" Jenna spoke barely above a whisper.

This time the girl looked up. Her eyes were sunken and hollow, her complexion sallow. "I know you." She said, more to convince herself than anything.

Jenna squatted closer. She could smell urine on the girl's clothing. "Where's Kyle? The police are looking for him."

Vicky rubbed a dirty hand across her nose. "Don't know. I rang his bell for the last couple of nights but he aint answering." She looked at Jenna defiantly. "I don't have a key to get in your building."

"So you do know who I am?" Jenna barked, "I was almost raped because of your boyfriend. He owes people money and they thought I was you."

Vicky rubbed her nose again, this time with the edge of her palm. "You're prettier than me."

Jenna ignored the comment. "The police are looking for Kyle and probably those two guys are too. Do you know them? Derek and Rashad?"

The girl scratched at her ankles. "Spare some change?"

Jenna wanted to shake her violently but the thought of touching the girl repulsed her. "Do you know where Kyle is?"

"I don't have a key and he didn't open the door. I went to the shelter but they wouldn't let me stay until I test clean. I been in the lobby of Longwharf but the manager is a real prick."

Jenna could tell she wasn't going to get anywhere with her line of questioning. A pang of sympathy shot through her as she recalled Edna's tale. She reached into her purse and dropped a ten dollar bill in the cup.

"I'm sorry for what they did to Kyle," she stated truthfully. "And I'm sorry you can't get back in the apartment." The last part, not so truthful. She was about to leave and head back to her friends when an idea crossed her mind.

"Vicky, did Kyle have a car? "

Vicky was too busy studying the bill that Jenna had presented.

Jenna tried something else. "Have you ever heard of John Robinson?"

A spark of life surfaced in Vicky Sue Robinson. "Course I do! Son of a bitch is my father!"

Pondering the little bit of information she had uncovered from Vicky, Jenna returned to the club just in time for Marta to hand her a two dollar shot. It came in a vial and was red. Marta couldn't provide further details.

"Just drink it Jennie. Ma told me we're singing after this cowboy finishes his song."

Jenna couldn't see the cowboy her girlfriend was referring to. All she heard was a strong masculine voice piping out the lyrics to "Ring of Fire."

"Where is Edna?" she asked.

Marta tore into a teriyaki skewer. "Flirting, dancing, who knows? It's too packed in here to find her."

The strains of the cowboy continued to echo through the room.

"Nice voice?" Marta noted.

Jenna agreed, but the voice did more than resonate with her. It was oddly familiar. She downed the test tube which she guessed contained Jaigermeister. " Whew! We have to stop mixing or I'll have a hangover for sure."

Chewing on the meat, Marta managed a reply. "I welcome a hangover. It will make Ma easier to deal with in the morning." She touched Jenna on the forearm. "She won't let me breathe since I got home. First, my checking account. She makes sure I bank two hundred dollars a week. If I buy something, she asks for the receipt."

"What's wrong with some sound financial advice?" Jenna defended. "Edna owns her own property and she hobnobs with big shot CEO's all day. You could do far worse."

"It's not that Jennie."

Jenna waited but when nothing came forth "Well then what?"

"It's just like Ma wants me to lead a storybook life. You know go to school, meet Prince Charming, get married and have four kids."

Jenna laughed. "And what does Marta want?"

Marta picked up another skewer. She hesitated and then handed it to Jenna. "You better eat this. I just smell food and I gain weight."

Jenna took the offer and wolfed it down, munching in rhythm to the cowboy's melodious tone. "God that's good! Anymore?"

"I ordered a half dozen and the one you saw me chewing was the only one I had."

"Edna!" Jenna accused. "How does she eat like a linebacker and look like a model?"

"Tell me about it," smirked Marta. "I'm afraid to bring a boy home. Once he lays eyes on Ma, I'm history."

Jenna took stock of her friend. It was true, she didn't match her mother's bombshell looks, but then again who did? Marta was a beautiful olive skinned girl, with an innocent face and a pleasant enough body to entice any future suitors. Her problem wasn't her mother at all. She had been shy in college, and it had carried over post-graduation.

"Marta, you could have any man you desire."

Just then the singing stopped. The cowboy was greeted with a raucous cheer as the karaoke conductor announced that Jenna and company would be on right after his bathroom break. Edna returned to the table, her face glowing with excitement.

"Wasn't he wonderful?" It was more of a statement than a question.

Marta could tell her mother was bursting with news. "Let me guess, ma. You snagged a date with him. Or did you just offer him a handjob in the bathroom?"

Edna grimaced. "You're disgusting. No wonder you're sitting here all alone."

Jenna cleared her throat. "Hello? Best friend sitting right next to her."

Edna's face brightened again. "That's why I rushed back. To tell you about the cowboy."

"What about him Edna?"

The sexy siren was about to reveal when the loudspeaker erupted.

"Next up we have the three amigas, Jennie, Edna and Marta," the karaoke presenter boomed.

"It will have to wait." Edna instructed. "It's our moment ladies."

Marta grabbed her hand and led her away from the table. Her shyness temporarily blinded by alcohol, the young Latina was ready for her spotlight.

It was then that he brushed by. The cowboy hat was pulled down low across his brow, but it did not hide the patch of freckles adorning his face. Jenna gasped. The voice had seemed familiar because she had heard it before. The would be Johnny Cash was none other than Sergeant Martin Conrad of the Boston Police Department.

"Marty!" Jenna cried out but the noise of the crowd drowned out her voice and her desired audience continued on his way out the exit.

"You saw?" Edna gulped in excitement jumping up and down. Her top threatened to come off. "It's a sign."

Jenna didn't answer. She was overcome with an odd sensation of dizziness and excitement, a case of the butterflies, her mom would say. Whatever it was, it filled her with confidence and she ran up to the podium with her friends in tow, a feeling of vigor running through her body.

«—»

Jenna awoke the next morning without any residual effects from the previous night's outing. Long ago she had learned that three aspirins and a tall glass of water before bed was prescription to avoid a nasty hangover. Marta hadn't been so lucky.

"Where you off to?" she asked, noticing Jenna had her gym bag slopped over a shoulder.

"Visiting Mr. Maxwell and then I'm headed home."

Marta had been heating up teriyaki in the toaster oven. They had ordered a full dozen before departing last night. "Did you tell Ma?"

Jenna nodded. "She wasn't too thrilled about it, but the locks have been changed and I don't think Kyle is stupid enough to show his face around the building anymore."

Marta opened the toaster oven and the aroma of salted meat flushed through the kitchen. "My head is still spinning. I don't know how Ma does it. She drank us under the table and she's probably halfway into her shift by now." She glanced at the clock. It was almost ten. "You can come back if it doesn't feel right."

Jenna came over and hugged her. "I know sweetie. I'll be ok."

Thirty minutes later, after a stop at Mike's Pastry, she was arriving in Post Office Square to visit hew new friend Grant Maxwell. He was the proprietor of a hole in the wall flower shop between Water and Broad Streets. She didn't know why he bothered to open on Saturdays, the district was deserted, devoid of foot traffic.

"Why not?" Grant Maxwell had told her. "What else do I have to do on Saturdays? My Linda is gone. Has been for close to fifteen years. I use to visit the cemetery but the last few times a couple of guys followed me with shovels."

Jenna laughed so hard she almost spilled her coffee. "Stop it Grant. You're not that old."

He waved her off. 'I have been in the flower business for as long as I can remember. It use to be when someone gave you flowers it meant I love you. Now it means I'm sorry… or forgive me, or I'm too lazy to drive to the mall." He plucked at the stem of a long rose. "There was a time when gentlemen gave these out for every occasion: a date, a thank you. Whatever. Now it's just birthdays and holidays."

"Yeah but you're still doing ok?" Jenna begged to know.

"Certainly, Gina," he replied with pride. She never corrected his mispronunciation of her name. "Morons come in here everyday and drop a hundred dollar bill on something that might last three days if lucky." He picked up his cannoli. Jenna had ordered him a Florentine with chocolate chips on both ends. "Heaven." He declared.

Jenna exchanged small talk and then related the events of the previous days. She omitted Crooked Teeth and Bill Esposito, those events seeming trivial in the wake of her apartment attack.

He gritted his teeth in anger. "Savages! There was a time when black kids couldn't walk the North End without drawing attention."

She ignored his racist comment. "I don't think I'll see them again. Edna really can swing a bat."

Grant Maxwell nodded his approval. "Lucky it wasn't me. I would have kept on hitting them." He took pause to daydream through that scenario. "What did your folks say?"

Jenna finished her coffee. "Didn't tell them."

"Why?" he demanded.

"My mom and dad are wonderful people, the best," she said sincerely. "I don't think I ever told you about them."

Grant shook his head and folded his hands together like a kindergarten student during story-time.

"I was a change of life baby," Jenna began. "My mother was forty-five years old when she had me. And Daddy, well he is eleven years older than her."

"Not spring chickens. " Grant intervened. "So you don't want to bother them? I get it."

Jenna nodded at his understanding. "They live in New Hampshire. Dad retired early from Westinghouse and since I'm an only child, they have no expenses."

"Lucky them. I have three children." He rolled his eyes. "Had three. My Rolf had a heart attack two years past. Left behind two children."

"Sorry," Jenna responded. "Do you see them often?"

He waved his arm in an arc around the store. "It's Saturday in June. What do you think? The mother brings them around during the holidays but that's it. My other two are no better."

Jenna decided to change the subject in an attempt to lighten the mood. "Well I'm here and I won't be ignored! How about walking me home?"

Grant Maxwell stood and took a bow. He handed her the long stem rose he had been fiddling with. "My lady, it would be a pleasure. I need to play my numbers anyway."

«—»

After a stop at the White Hen, Grant Maxwell had insisted they head over to Bricco where he purchased fresh bread for both of them. Naturally, he refused her money. She had enjoyed his company, especially his gallantry. The stubborn old man demanded to walk her up the stairs despite her protestations.

He left her with a kiss on the cheek, a faint touch of Old Spice wafting from his pores. It delighted her to know such a wonderful person.

Once inside, she tossed her bag on the sofa and placed the rose in a tall glass with water. Her thoughts drifted toward her parents as she opened a window to let the stifled air out. Maybe Grant Maxwell was right. Maybe she should have told them what happened. But she knew her Dad too well. He would insist she move back home immediately. And Mom? She'd make Edna Ruiz look tame by comparison. Mom didn't even trust doctors. No man but your husband should see your God given form.

Jenna giggled. "Oh Mom, if you only knew." Visions of Martin Conrad sporting the cowboy hat, his hand gripping the brim in acknowledgement of the crowd's cheers, danced through her mind. A wave of desire flowed through her.

The doorbell rang.

Panic gripped Jenna. Her eyes frantically sought the baseball bat Edna had used on her culprits, but she couldn't recall where she had placed it.

She ran to the window to see who it was but the person was blocked by the building's awning. She breathed deeply a couple of times.

"The foyer is locked." She reminded herself. "They can't get in without a key."

Derek and Rashad didn't let that stop them. She reached for the phone to call 911 but then thought better of it. "Probably Edna come to demand I go home with her again."

Resolving to not let her fear rule her, Jenna descended the stairs and peered into the peephole. To her relief it was a uniformed FedEx driver. He had a look of permanent impatience.

"Delivery," he yelled, sensing her.

Jenna swung open the door and snatched the package.

"Please sign," the driver demanded.

She did as was requested and was about to slam the door on him when she spotted a familiar face standing at the base of the stairs. It was Vicky, still dressed in the clothes from the night before. Every instinct commanded Jenna to shut the door, but she couldn't.

"Thank you," said the FedEx driver in a robotic tone. He departed without looking back.

"What do you want?" Jenna asked ice in her tone.

Vicky moved forward a couple of steps. "Please, I have no place to go."

Jenna stood rigid. "Go home. Go to Salem. "

"I can't," Vicky replied, her tone sober. "I haven't been back there in a longtime. Not since Kyle and my father fought."

Not my problem, Jenna tried to invoke. What came out instead was "Can't you go somewhere else?"

Vicky moved closer, her breath giving off an awful stench. Jenna could tell she hadn't brushed in a while. "I don't want to go to a shelter. The last time they stole my phone and my I.D. card."

Suddenly the FedEx box felt like it weighed a thousand pounds. Against all her better judgement, Jenna found herself uttering the unthinkable. "You can come in until we straighten this out."

The first thing Jenna did was demand the girl take a bath. Between the heat and lack of air conditioning, Vicky was ripe.

Reluctant to leave her alone, Jenna helped the girl undress. She was shocked when she peeled the girl's grungy shirt off. Underneath, her bra was soiled and yellow, but this was not the most disturbing thing. There were cigarette burns all over her stomach.

"Kyle?" Jenna whispered in a terrified tone.

Vicky just shook her head. "No, Kyle never hurt anyone."

Jenna had retrieved a brown shopping back from the kitchen. She pinched two fingers together and picked up the girl's t-shirt. She threw it in the bag. "Your clothes have to go," she stated. "You can borrow some of mine while you're here."

Vicky nodded, showing more signs of stability than she had expressed outside the Blue Line Station last night. She dropped her bra into the bag, and then proceeded to remove her stretch pants and underwear from her body.

Her bottom half didn't fail to shock either. There were black and blues on both thighs.

"Vicky, who did this?" Jenna demanded.

The girl didn't answer. She just scooped up the clothing and placed it in the bag with the rest of her stuff. She removed her socks and stepped into the warm bath.

Jenna decided not to press the issue. Something about this frumpy girl's plight struck a cord in her. She wet a face cloth and dipped it in the water and gently cleaned the girl's back. The water turned dark immediately.

"Thank you," Vicky croaked. Her voice far older than her actual age. "You don't have to stay here with me." She paused, frowning. "I'm not going to rifle through your medicine cabinet."

"Wouldn't do you any good unless you like Midol." Jenna stated. "Let me get you a robe."

Jenna departed the bathroom but left the door ajar. She retreated to the living room to examine the FedEx package.

Wonder what this is?

The return address wasn't recognizable. Curious, she ripped open the box. It contained a gift basket of cheese and crackers, courtesy of the ever guilty Mr. William Esposito.

"Seriously?" she spoke aloud.

In his attempt to make amends, William Esposito was becoming an even further disappointment. She tossed the package on the kitchen table and went to retrieve a bath robe for her guest.

Vicky Sue Robinson gnawed on the cheese and crackers with vigor. Jenna could tell she had been hungry. "Slow down. You might choke."

"Sorry," Vicky said, leaning back on the sofa. The fluffy bathrobe dwarfed her tiny frame, making her seem younger than she was. "I didn't mean to make a mess."

Jenna smiled politely. She studied the girl closely.

Vicky had cleaned up well. Her strands of long black hair shone nicely after a triple shampoo wash, and her face looked softer and less weary. Jenna actually felt guilty about her previous opinions of the young woman.

"How come you can't go home to Salem?" she asked.

Vicky looked as if she had just discovered a case of constipation. "That old bastard."

"Your father? John?"

Vicky nodded, fixing herself another cracker with blueberry goat cheese. "He did this to me." She opened the bathrobe to reveal the burns below her tiny breasts.

Jenna swallowed back a scream. She had never been subjected to such physical abuse. The only other person she knew who had suffered such trauma was Edna.

How could he do such a thing? To his own daughter?

Vicky folded the flap of the robe back over her exposed skin.

It was clear Jenna had treaded on private property. "I'm sorry Vicky. How old are you?"

"Nineteen."

Jenna was taken aback. She had mistaken the girl for being closer to thirty. Obviously, the hard life was taking its toll. "Does your mom know this is going on?"

"Maybe." Vicky replied nonchalantly. "If you believe in the afterlife and all that. Mom died when I was young. Car accident. No mystery about it or anything. One day she left for work and never came back."

Jenna teared up. She was remembering Edna's confession from last night. She felt even more remorse at being so angry with Vicky. "Your dad took it hard?"

"What do you think? He had just started his family. He had a little girl to take care of and a wife to bury. It didn't take long before booze became his only friend." She stood up and headed to the window, her tiny body casting a shadow on the wall. "I thought things would be different when we moved to Salem. Grandpa and Grandma gave us the house. They thought dad could handle it. All he had to do was pay taxes and utilities. The mortgage was paid in full."

"What happened?" Jenna inquired, her own appetite squashed.

"Daddy got worse. He quit his job at the bank or so he said. Grandpa thinks he was fired. Then he just fueled up on hard stuff for as long as I can recall. Just recently he got into towing, and that's how I met Kyle."

So Kyle does work! Or did. Jenna recorded to herself.

Vicky continued. "They made a good team. Daddy would hitch up the cars and Kyle would keep the lookout."

"Repo men."

Yep. Good business. Especially the last few years. They couldn't keep up with the calls. Most of the jobs came in the low income neighborhoods, Roxbury, Chelsea. That's when Kyle met Derek and Rashad."

Anger seeped into Jenna again. "Last night you told me you didn't know them."

Vicky turned away from the window. "Last night I was high. I couldn't wipe my own butt."

I noticed, Jenna thought. In a civil tone, she announced. "They attacked me."

"I know. Word spread fast. "She came over and sat on the sofa with Jenna. "They hurt Kyle too."

Jenna nodded. "I'm sorry. Kyle was a quiet neighbor. He didn't deserve that."

Vicky shocked her with her reply. "Kyle is an opportunist. I'm just a friend with benefits to him. I wish my father had never met him."

Jenna didn't know how to respond. Her saccharine tainted world read like a kid's Golden story book. She had seen life through rose colored lenses. She stared at this burn riddled girl in front of her, four years younger and already bearing a backlog of grief that could kickstart a Lifetime movie.

"You know he owes those guys a lot of money," she said.

Vicky bit her lower lip in thought. "Derek and Rashad are creeps but they ain't the real thing. They've just watched Scarface too many times."

Jenna didn't believe that for a minute. "Did you know them well?"

"Never actually met them."

The words resonated in her ears.

Jenna got up and removed the cheese tray. She went into the kitchen and covered it with saran wrap, her mind spinning in a dozen directions. Her thoughts kept returning to the license plate number. It seemed innocent now. Kyle was in the tow truck business. It stood to reason that he would deal with plate numbers all day long. But why John Robinson, his business partner? And why write it down?

She took a stab in the dark.

"Vicky, you said there has been some problems with your father and you because of Kyle?"

"Yes. That's why he threw this beating on me. I thought at first it was just another night with his friend Jim Beam, but then he started yelling that Kyle ripped him off and that if I saw him I was to tell him daddy was on the warpath. That's what I planned to do the other night before Derek and Rashad worked him over, but I haven't seen him since."

A look of realization dawned on her. "Jenna, do you think my dad is behind this?"

"I don't know. Maybe we should pay your dad a visit."

Vicky blinked twice. "You want to do what?"

"Tomorrow. Let's visit your dear old dad." She stated boldly, trying to convince herself that it was a good idea.

Vicky shrugged. "Well, if you are going to see that bastard, Sunday is the best time. They don't sell booze on Sunday."

«—»

"I wish my father had never met him."

"Out of the question!" Edna Ruiz shouted into the phone receiver. "Especially with that little puta in my car!"

Jenna had just explained her desire to trek out to Salem and had asked Edna for a ride.

"I'm taking you back to MGH!" Edna exclaimed. "I can't believe you were stupid enough to let that skank sleepover. She could have cut your throat while you slept."

Jenna still remained quiet, letting her friend vent.

"I thought my daughter was thick in the head. You take the cake. Today is my only day off. My answer is no. No! No! No!"

An hour later, Edna and Marta pulled up in front of Jenna's apartment on Prince Street. Her green Kia Solo idling, Edna beeped twice and rolled down the window. "Let's go before I change my mind!"

Salem, Massachusetts is a historic down, with a charming waterfront and a thriving tourist trade. One of the most beautiful places on the planet, it's a vacationers dream site, but only blocks away from the high priced hotels and costly yachts can be found one of the ugliest blighted ghettos one could ever expect to lay eyes on. This is where those lovely tax dollars that flowed into the city ended up in a sprawling section of overcrowded brick tenement housing units.

Fortunately for Vicky she had been raised on the other side of the city that abutted the even richer town of Beverly. Elm Street was right on the border of both towns, a desirable and pleasant neighborhood.

Unfortunately, the Robinson house seemed out of place in this well kept neighborhood. Vicky's father had let it rundown horribly. The paint was peeling and the grass high and un-mowed. The roof was in a state of despair, making one wonder if it leaked.

Edna pulled up past it and parked at the corner of the next street.

"There was room in the driveway for your car." Vicky said. She looked clownish in the blouse and jeans she had borrowed from Jenna. The clothing fit well enough around the hips and arms, but the sleeves and pant legs were way too long for her frame. She had rolled up the jeans as best as she could.

"I don't want to be parked in your driveway if something goes wrong," Edna barked. She wore dark sunglasses which she removed. "I don't feel good about this."

"Jennie just wants to get some answers, Ma," retorted Marta. She stepped out of the car into the warm air. She was dressed casually in a t-shirt and denim shorts.

Jenna wore similar attire. "She's right Edna," she got out and pulled Vicky with her. "I just want to help Vicky straighten this out with her dad."

Edna sighed and stepped out from the driver's side. She was decked out with flare in a pair of skintight orange bike shorts with an over-sized white Mickey Mouse t-shirt. She donned the glasses again. "You should have let me bring the bat."

"Maybe this is a bad idea," Vicky offered.

Jenna was resolved for a confrontation. "No, we're going to check this out." She rang the doorbell and waited. A minute passed without a response.

"No one's home. Let's go," said Edna. She tugged at Jenna.

Jenna ignored her and wrapped on the door firmly. The tin number nine that was nailed to the door fell off in response. Still no one answered.

"The tow truck is gone," Vicky said. "He may be on a call or out."

Not to be deterred, Jenna looked around. Her gaze fell to the driveway where a dilapidated garage stood. She strolled over and pressed her face against a pane of glass.

"Bingo!" she exalted.

The object of her excitement was a mid- nineties Chevy Malibu bearing the license ZDV14K.

She yanked at the garage door but it would not budge. "Damn!"

Edna was furious. "Damn is right. Now you're trying your luck at B&E? What the hell is wrong with you?"

Marta looked frightened. "For once I agree with Ma. Let's go."

No one had noticed that Vicky had disappeared. She had gone into the backyard, a labyrinth of uncut grass and lawn debris. She returned holding something in her hand.

"What is it?" Edna demanded. "Answer me you little turd!"

Tensions were definitely building. Jenna tried to defuse the situation. "This won't take long. Edna why don't you and Marta go get the car. I'll open the garage with Vicky and we'll be right there."

Marta shook her head cautiously. "No Jennie. Let's just go!"

Edna didn't prolong the discussion. She grasped a firm hand on her daughter's shoulder and marched back in the direction of the car.

"I'm sorry for angering your friend," said Vicky. "I know how crazy Spanish chicks can get."

Jenna said nothing. She inserted the key and turned the knob. The latch unlocked and a moment later they were inside the musty garage. A rodent or a squirrel exited on the left, too quickly for either girl to notice.

"It's locked," Vicky noticed.

Jenna didn't know what came over her. She reacted without hesitation. Picking up a three pronged pitchfork, she struck the window as hard as she could with the wooden end. Glass shattered and sprayed all over the driver's seat. Vicky said nothing. In fact, she was calm. She pushed Jenna out of the way and reached in the door handle and popped the trunk. Dust sprayed as the hatch popped open, and then they both peered in. Much to their dismay it contained only a box of paperbacks, graphic novels actually.

"Those are Kyle's," Vicky stated briefly. "He don't read too much but a couple years back he bought all those at the sidewalk sale at Harrison's."

Jenna realized she had been holding her breath. Too many movies. She told herself. She had been expecting a corpse or a murder weapon or something, not a box of Marvel comics. She picked one up and blew the dust off its cover,

"Essential Tales of the Zombie," she read aloud. How in the world could that be essential? She flipped through the pages when something green fell out.

Vicky scooped it up immediately. "That pothead Kyle. Look what he used as a bookmark. What a lack of brains."

Jenna ignored her. She was leafing through the rest of the book locating more of the so called bookmarks.

"Unreal!" She grabbed the box and turned to Vicky. "Let's go."

Vicky nodded, still clutching the hundred dollar bill.

Jenna and Vicky agreed that it was prudent not to share news of their discovery with the Ruiz women. This proved a wise decision. Edna and Marta concluded they would salvage what was left of the weekend with a trip to Piers Park. It was obvious their invitation extended only to Jenna, the distrust and dislike for Vicky not hidden at all. Jenna politely declined the offer and was relieved when her friends had finally dropped them back off in the North End.

"Those girls can't stand me," Vicky said. It wasn't a question or an accusation, simply a fact, one which sounded as if it had been uttered many times in the past.

Jenna ignored her, focusing on the haul they had recovered. After going through the entire box of books, she had counted over four hundred bills, all of them sporting the glorious image of Benjamin Franklin. Forty thousand dollars! She pondered what to do.

Usually, she would turn to streetwise Edna, but not today with the mood she was in. The police were an option, but after considering it she had nagging fears that the situation could escalate beyond her control. After all, they had broken into the Robinson garage and destroyed property. Even if the money didn't belong to Vicky's father, the law would see things quite differently.

Vicky had stripped down to a camisole and tap set which Jenna had loaned her. Sweat was pouring from her tiny frame causing the clothing to cling to her. Jenna could make out her pubic mound beneath the satin bottoms.

"You ok?" she asked the girl.

"Not sure." Vicky answered. "I think I have sunstroke. " Her long black hair was plastered to her scalp.

Jenna moved the fan over to the sofa. "You better lay down. Let me get you a pillow." From the hall closet she removed a pillow buddy with the design of Belle from Beauty and the Beast on it. It had been a gift from her dad which she treasured. It had even survived the keg party days at Stonehill.

"I feel like crap," Vicky noted, tremors running up and down her spine.

"I'm going to fix us a sandwich," Jenna offered. She went into the kitchen and quickly opened a can of Bumblebee tuna which she poured into a bowl and added mayonnaise. She served it warm on thin slices of the Bricco bread that Grant Maxwell had purchased for her.

Vicky chewed slowly, swallowing by force. The sweat continued to drip from her frame soaking her top completely. Her knees buckled. "You better get me a bucket – fast!"

Jenna had experienced this routine many times at college. She flew across the room and grabbed the short waste paper basket she had picked up from Bed Bath and Beyond. She emptied its contents on the floor and handed it to Vicky just in the nick of time.

The girl heaved violently, flecks of tuna hanging from her chin.

"Oh god!" realization had struck Jenna. "You're having withdrawal!"

It was over quickly and Jenna was thankful the youth hadn't lost control of her bowels as some junkies were want to do. She wet a face cloth and wiped the remnants from Vicky's face. "You'll be alright."

Vicky clutched at the pillow, tears streaming down her cheeks. "Don't throw me out. Please!"

The thought had never crossed Jenna's mind. She sought only to soothe the girl's pain.

"I won't leave you, I promise."

Jenna plunked down on the sofa, the pillow buddy on her lap. Vicky curled up next to her, squeezing her entire body onto one cushion and clutching at Jenna's thigh. She thrashed back and forth.

"Stay still Vicky," Jenna mustered up as much authority as she dared. She feared the girl might lash out at her, but Vicky was too tired and dehydrated to put up a struggle.

"Don't hit me again, daddy!" she begged. She tugged at the camisole, her burn marks evident beneath. "I'll fix you another drink."

She was hallucinating. It frightened Jenna even more. "No one will hurt you Vicky. I promise."

Vicky ripped the camisole from her body and began to rub at her wounds. "It hurts. Give me the pill to make it better. Please!"

"No more pills Vicky." Jenna pushed her back down, the girl's naked torso landing on the pillow. "Just stay still and I'll help you get through it."

"Okay Jenna." Was all the girl could spit out before her eyes rolled back and she collapsed.

Jenna hugged her tightly, rocking the small girl's frame in her arms. "How could anybody do this to a teenager?"

Her mind was resolved. Time to call in the calvalry. Careful not to jostle Vicky she reached on the end table for her purse. She needed the business card for Martin Conrad. He would know what to do.

Martin Conrad was all business upon arrival. He instructed Jenna to fill the bath tub with cold water and ice cubes. He then carried the half-naked Vicky into the bath room and submerged her into the icy bath. He checked her airway for possible signs of blockage.

"Why didn't you tell me it was this bad?" he barked. "This woman needs an ambulance."

The sergeant's stern tone hurt Jenna but she accepted his admonishment. "I thought she had just passed out from the heat but then she started shaking and throwing up, and…" Jenna couldn't finish. She reached into the cold water to grab Vicky's hand. "She's so young. Is she going to die?"

He lifted his broad shoulders and turned to her. Their eyes locked. "Not on my watch. "The words came out with such reassurance that Jenna felt a small victory in her decision to call him.

She stood back and let him call it in on his radio. Jenna was so enthralled in the moment that she failed to notice he was out of uniform.

"They'll be here in a minute."

Jenna placed a hand on the prone girl's cheek. "What will happen to her?"

"She's going to get the help she needs," he stood up. "Is there family that needs to be contacted?"

Jenna's mind drifted back to the rundown house on Elm Street. "No, she's been living across the way with her boyfriend. There's no one else," she lied.

Jenna had ridden in the ambulance with Vicky, Martin Conrad trailing behind in his own vehicle. The whole process flew by in a blur, only one thought crowding Jenna's mind.

"Let her live God. Let her live."

Vicky had been transported and admitted into the Faulkner Hospital in Jamaica Plain, a mecca for drug rehabilitation. A few hours had passed after the harrowing events inside her apartment, and it was only now that she felt her friend was out of danger.

"Friend?"

Yes, the girl who use to annoy her with the clankety rolling suitcase each weekend had come to mean something to Jenna. She couldn't really explain it to herself, but the feelings were there. This troubled teen who had endured far too much in her brief time on the planet had somehow carved a niche in Jenna's heart.

"Hungry?" Marty Conrad broke up her thoughts.

Jenna nodded. She had expected to eat a tuna sandwich before Vicky's breakdown, but it hadn't come to pass. She felt her stomach rumble.

"Me too, " spoke the thick necked officer. "My roommate must be starving by now."

Jenna felt a sharp pang. "Girlfriend?"

"No, not Chuck. But he nags like one if I come home late."

She smiled, hoping her relief didn't show. "And where is home, Sergeant Conrad?"

"Charlestown. "

"I thought only bad guys live in Charlestown?" Jenna kidded. "Isn't that what Hollywood preaches?"

"You'd be surprised," he answered. "Residency law requires all BPD personnel live within city limits for the first ten years of employment. So I guess that means I'll be a nearby neighbor for the next half dozen years or so."

I hope so," she thought. "Shouldn't you call Chuck and let him know you're bringing home a dinner guest?"

He let loose with a quick laugh. "No, he never answers the phone. And besides, I pay the entire rent. "

"So I'm not the only one giving out free lodging?" she joked.

"Be careful Ms. Coyne. It's my professional opinion that people enjoy your company."

He's flirting!

"You be careful too Sergeant Conrad. It's my professional opinion that people enjoy your singing."

A look of confusion drifted over his face, erased by a wide grin. "You were there!" He challenged. "Truth is, I have a great memory, and I do recall the young Ms. Ruiz in her statement claiming you folks had plans to go to the Hong Kong before those jerks ruined your night."

"Yeah, but how'd you know I'd go back last night?"

"I didn't," he laughed. "I just imagined it was like a stakeout. I was going to sing every night until you appeared."

"The singing cowboy, huh?"

"That's me," his smile was contagious. "We really have to go or Chuck will trash the place."

"Ok, you saved Vicky from trashing my place, let me return the favor."

Chuck, the roommate, was actually a Jack Russell terrier who had been found last year in a car with the windows rolled up. Martin Conrad had followed through with the case, intrigued by the small canine who ended up in a kennel at the city's animal shelter. He had been scheduled for euthanization, when Sergeant Conrad saved his life a second time by adopting him.

Sometimes, Marty wished he had never made that decision.

The place looked like someone had broken in and trashed it. Newspaper pages were strewn across the floor, and a basket of laundry had been overturned and its contents scattered around.

"Thanks, Chuck."

Jenna kneeled to pet the feisty animal. His coat was mostly white with touches of brown around the ears. He yipped twice at her before sniffing her flip flops. "He's adorable," she proclaimed.

"Don't flatter him. He'll be bossing you around too."

She smacked her lips together at the dog. "Not Chuck. He's too precious."

The dog continued to circle her, thrilled to have a visitor.

Martin Conrad drew open a cupboard and pulled down two wine glasses. "I have to admit at first I suspected he was abused or just plain retarded," he confessed. "I couldn't figure out why he didn't understand me."

He placed the long stem glasses down and uncorked a bottle of merlot. "I'd ask him to sit or fetch or do any number of simple things and he'd just stare at me." He poured two healthy sized glasses. "I even contemplated that he might be deaf."

Jenna took the glass from him and clinked it against his own. "But what did your detective skills discover?"

He sipped the merlot. "Well, I'm not a detective, not yet anyway, but I'm a damn good cop and after a few days I did crack the case."

Jenna reached down, patted Chuck again. "And what was this handsome creature's crime?"

"That's just it. No crime at all. Chuck isn't stupid or deaf," he paused, " wait for it… he's Spanish!"

"What?"

"That was my response too but watch I can prove it." He moved into the living room and flipped on his old fashioned Panasonic TV. It was the heavy kind that weighed a ton and didn't play HD channels. He turned on the ten o'clock news and waited.

"Is this the part where you amaze me like David Copperfield?" Jenna smirked.

Martin Conrad shook his head. "That's the rub. That's the gag. See him." He pointed at Chuck who was sitting in the living room gnawing on a sock that had apparently occupied the laundry basket. "Look no response at all to the TV."

Jenna waited. "Yeah?"

"Now watch." The sergeant punched in the code for Univision. A commercial was playing. He upped the volume a bit.

Chuck stopped playing with the sock and in one bound landed on the coffee table. His attention was focused squarely on the monitor.

"Oh my God, that's funny," proclaimed Jenna.

"Yeah but watch this." Marty swapped back to the other channel, a rerun of Magnum PI blared from the speaker. Chuck leaped down from the coffee table and resumed dabbling with the dirty laundry. "And again," Martin announced, switching back to Univision. The dog became alert again and claimed his prime viewing spot on the coffee table.

"Must have belonged to a Latino family," said Jenna.

Marty nodded. "Leaves me only two options. Either I retrain him in English or I start learning Spanish."

Jenna gulped more of her wine. She glanced over at a three shelved bookcase. The top two shelves contained hardcover books, most of them true crime annals. The bottom shelf was filled with old vhs cartridges and a small framed photo.

The tapes were entirely cataloged of old b-movie westerns, all black and white, and all an hour or so long. The photo was of a uniformed officer and an old timer garbed in black cowboy gear. The photo appeared to be decades old.

"That's Pops," he supplied. "He was a cop too. That picture was taken before I was born."

"And the cowboy?" she asked.

Martin Conrad picked up the photo and handed it to her. "The cowboy was Lash Larue. Pops met him at the Bayside Expo center in the 1980's. Nowadays we'd get in trouble for getting photographed in our blues, but things were more lenient back then."

"Are the tapes his also?"

"They were. Pops was a big fan of the old matinee cowboys, Roy Rogers, Gene Autry, Hopalong Cassidy.. those guys. My mother said he practically wore out the VCR playing those things." He ran a finger across the top of the tape boxes, picking up a small amount of dust. "I should take better care of these."

Jenna could sense the sorrow in his tone. "Is your Pops still with us?"

He didn't turn around. She was almost happy about that. "I was five when it happened."

"Was he killed while serving?"

"Yes, he died in the line of duty." He finally turned around. She had been expecting tears, but the big man flashed a smile instead. "I'd love to tell you Pops died saving people in a gunfight or stopping a holdup or something but the truth is just plain boring. He was killed working a detail shift." He drained the remainder of his wine and headed into the kitchen for a refill. "Some guy took the corner too fast, saw the blue sawhorse and then swerved into my Pops. He didn't have a chance."

He refilled her glass, adding a little bit more this time. "I remember Joe coming over that night to tell us. My mother didn't cry or anything. She just thanked him, made dinner for us, and later that night right before bed she called me and my sister Annie and told us Pops had died that day."

Jenna held back her tears. She almost felt guilty for her own life, devoid of such heartbreak.

"Was Joe his partner?"

"Yes, and he also became my stepfather." Marty threw back a long slug of the hot wine. "It's not as uncommon as you think in my line of duty. Police communities are tight knit, and from grief stems comfort and compassion. Even young guys I know on the force have similar stories." He washed down the rest of his glass. "Anyway, Joe is a good man, a hellava husband for my mom and a good father to my three younger brothers... and myself." He tipped the glass toward his father's photo. "But Pops will always be my hero."

"And you will always be mine." Jenna placed her glass down and ran a fingertip up and down his chest. Martin Conrad took the hint. He gathered her in his arms and kissed her gently. She returned the gesture with zest.

"Still hungry?" He whispered.

"Oh, yes."

A silver tow truck pulled in front of Simcoe's hot dog stand on Blue Hill Avenue in Mattapan. Its single occupant exited the car, a giant of a man. His bald head adorned with the image of an American eagle and his arms covered in tattooed sleeves displaying various jungle animals. He wore dark sunglasses and a sleeveless motorcycle vest over a plain white t-shirt, his look completed with faded jeans and construction boots. He sported a soul patch on his chin and a dour frown to match. John Robinson was the poster child for trouble.

The object of his attention was a young black youth departing the establishment with two of the famous foot long dogs in his hands. The kid wore a Los Angeles Kings hockey jersey size 4X, even though he had the frame of a string bean.

It was eleven o'clock on a fine Monday morning.

"Those look tasty, Derek." The man's booming voice matched his exterior. It was gruff and demanding, a hint of violence behind each syllable.

Derek played it cool.

"What up John, where's Kyle?" he asked nonchalantly. When the big man didn't answer, Derek calmly offered one of his hot dogs. "Try this man. Best dog in the city."

John Robinson accepted the handout and placed it on the hood of his vehicle. The rusty old truck screamed to tell a million tales. Most of them would end up unpleasant for someone.

"I was hoping you could tell me. Seems you boys paid him a visit last weekend. Ain't no one heard or seen him since." His tone was civil, not accusatory. "Something go down?"

Derek wasn't a fool. He knew John Robinson wouldn't have driven all the way down from Salem on a weekday if he didn't already know what had happened so he decided to lay it out.

"Look man, you run a business. Me and Shad, we run a business. Kyle owes us some serious cash so we paid him a visit, slapped him around a bit."

Robinson stood still, arms folded, massive biceps flexing. "I understand business, Derek. And I won't stand up for Kyle. The little prick is as useless as tits on a bull. That being said, you still deprived me of an asset and that has to be compensated for."

Derek said nothing. He knew he was no match for the burly giant.

"Here's how this going to play out," Robinson continued. "I'll replace Kyle. God knows that snot brought nothing but trouble into my life but you have to help me out. One day of repo work, starting now."

Derek shook his head back and forth. "You being fair I'll admit, but today is Monday, drop off day. Me and Shad have to run down to New Bedford and then we start the door to door as soon as it gets dark."

John Robinson removed his sunglasses. His eyes were cold and barren. "Derek, did you just tell me to go fuck myself? Cuz that's what I heard. Go fuck yourself John!"

"No, man. Not like that at all. I just want to postpone until tomorrow."

"See, there you go swearing at me again."

John Robinson grabbed the youth by the wrist and started to squeeze. Agony shot throughout Derek's body and he dropped his hotdog. The giant didn't loosen his grip. Instead, he held firmly while his other hand scooped up the fallen dog. It was loaded with chili and mustard.

"Poor baby. You dropped this." He smeared the hot dog and its toppings all over Derek's white hockey jersey.

Derek tried to yank his arm away to no avail. "Look man. I'm sorry we messed your boy and his girl up. But they owe us four grand."

John Robinson released his grip, stunned by the words he heard. "What did you say?"

"Four grand that white punk owe us."

Without hesitation, Robinson grabbed the arm again and slammed Derek down onto the hood of the truck. "Never mind that you black bastard. What did you say about the girl?"

Derek winced in pain, his face burning on the hot metal. "It was nothing man. Nothing. We just threatened the bitch. People told us he loved that little whore Vicky."

Robinson said nothing, his face turning red with anger. Instead he let his actions speak with devastating consequences. He drove an elbow into the back of Derek's neck. The sickening crunch of bone on metal left an indentation on the hood of the truck. Derek's unconscious form slid to the ground, where the angry behemoth kicked it and rolled it out of his way.

Calmly, he restored his sunglasses and reentered his vehicle. He slowly backed out of the parking slot and headed back down Blue Hill Avenue in the direction of Dorchester, his focus squarely centered on giving Rashad and equal share of attention.

Jenna's early morning had passed without incident. An early phone call confirmed Vicky's condition was improving. However, the staff nurse was adamant about no visitors, not yet at any rate, which suited Jenna fine. The young girl had given her the scare of a lifetime.

The silver lining, of course, was that Martin Conrad had made an impact on her life. She was still reveling in the joy of their evening encounter, hoping beyond all, that their relationship would continue. She had been bursting at the seams to reveal the encounter to her best friend Marta.

"I'm so happy for you Jennie," the round faced girl voiced on the other line. "These last couple of days have been so frightening, something good had to come out of it." She was on one of her fifteen minute union sanctioned breaks. "Ma was so pissed at you yesterday."

"I know." There was a hint of guilt and sorrow in Jenna's voice. "I thought she was going to burst a blood vessel."

Marta's voice began to rise. "Tell me about it. She came home, changed into her big mom jeans, and pouted the rest of the day. She kept on screaming that Vicky is the devil and she would corrupt you." There was a moment of silence. "Please tell me she's finally gone?"

"She isn't here anymore." Jenna neglected to mention the seizure episode. "She left last night."

"Thank God," Marta's voice dripped with relief. "I never liked her since the first time I heard her big mouth outside your place. I hope that boyfriend of hers' is gone too."

Jenna cast a glance at the box of graphic novels and their hidden contents. She had hoped to hide it with the Ruiz, but this telephone conversation axed any notions of the idea. "I have a few days to myself, Marta. I think I'll put them to good use looking for a new job."

"I can think of better ways to spend your time."

"You're talking about Marty?"

Marta let out a whoop. "It's Marty now is it? Not Officer Conrad? No wait, I mean Sergeant Conrad?" She sighed. "I guess I'll be seeing less of you now?"

"Never, I ..."

"I'm just kidding Jennie. Give me a call tomorrow. Ma and I are going to wine making class tonight."

Jenna brightened. "Can't wait to taste it. Love you."

"Love you too."

Jenna glanced at the cardboard box. "Now what?"

Kyle checked his cell phone once more. It was noon, on a Monday. There would be no better time to retrieve the cash than now. His employer, John Robinson, was a creature of habit. The brawny giant never missed lunch, even if it meant rescheduling a repo. Come hell or high water, twelve o'clock was lunch time. And there was no reason to believe today would be any different. So it was with supreme confidence that Kyle entered the garage on Elm street.

The surprise awaiting him was not to his liking one little bit.

"Shit!!!" His heart skipped a beat. "Shit, shit, shit!" His voice echoed as he popped the button to release the trunk latch. As he had suspected, the box was gone.

Despair crumpled his knees.

"Shit! Shit! Shit!"

"Forty thousand dollars! Gone!"

One of the perks of being in the tow business is that the customer is taken by surprise. No one plans on breaking down or being repossessed. And in many cases the owner isn't even present at the time of the hitch up. This unpleasant truth resulted in a bonus for the tow truck driver.

Not all drivers took advantage of their customers, but John Robinson was such a man. In addition to the meager salary he paid Kyle, he had offered him a unique incentive plan. Kyle could keep whatever he found in the trunk or backseats of the unsuspecting suckers who had the bad luck to make the short list of non-paying owners.

Three weeks ago John Robinson had received an order to repossess a 2014 Toyota Prius from an apartment building in Revere. Everything had gone according to schedule and before the car was returned to the lender, Kyle had ransacked the trunk.

Much to his chagrin, he uncovered a plain brown shopping back filled with four hundred immaculately sorted bills, all sporting the welcomed image of Benjamin Franklin. Kyle had kept his composure, shrugging off his boss's inquiries by simply reporting his find to be old work shirts.

"Maybe next time, kid," was all John Robinson had to offer.

Kyle had taken the money home at first, counted it carefully, and then had given it some thought. He couldn't tell Vicky, she'd tell her rotten old man. And he knew splitting it with John Robinson was out of the question. The barbaric man would never have gone for the idea. Kyle had concluded that the best plan was to hide the money until he could figure out how to spend it. He knew the North End apartment was out of the question. Vicky was too clever and the place saw a lot of foot traffic. He decided the best place to hide it was in plain sight. That's how he came up with the idea to load the bills in between the pages of his trade paperbacks. No one would ever look through those. And then it had dawned on him to place the money inside the garage, more specifically inside the rusting wreck that it encased.

The old Chevy Malibu had belonged to Vicky's mother. It stood as a memorial and a testament to the last shred of humanity somehow nestled deep in the bowels of John Robinson. He never used it, and he never let anyone touch it. The car was the perfect spot to hide the stash. Or so he had thought. Now, looking into the space vacated by the box, Kyle could only repeat one thought.

"Shit."

«—»

Rashad slammed his burner phone to the ground in disgust. It hit the soft turf once and bounced a few inches away. He was at Towne Park, situated in the heart of Fields Corner, a low income neighborhood in the urban section of Boston. It was getting late, and his supplier had just notified him that things were getting antsy in New Bedford. Derek and he were already two hours late for the Monday evening pickup. "Where are you?" His foot kicked at the disposable phone, willing it to ring. But no such luck.

The park was filled with spectators watching a Babe Ruth league game. Normal crowd for a normal afternoon in June. This was how Rashad liked it, out in the open, no back alleys or dark hallways where danger lurked. The drug business had no code of honor, and Rashad trusted no one, not even his cousin Derek. "Did that mofo go down there by himself this week?" The notion was improbable but not impossible. When Kyle had first started slacking on his payments, Rashad immediately suspected his cousin of some backdoor shadiness. Turned out he was wrong, of course. Kyle and his heroin junkie girlfriend Vicky had just decided to shoot up the profit, but in the back of his mind Rashad was still plagued by doubt.

"Maybe Derek has grown a pair? Maybe he is branching out?" He felt his fury starting to surface, and the he thought of his aunt, Derek's mother and her constant words of advice.

"Never go out alone. No black man should walk without an escort. Stay in a pack, like wolves. Strength in numbers." She had always preached. Solid words, from a trustful source.

Rashad didn't notice the car door open on the tow truck parked across the way in the strip mall. If he had looked that way, he would have seen big John Robinson emerge from his silver tow truck, peeling black cat logo on its doors. As it was, he spotted him too late.

"Thought I'd find you here," the burly giant barked.

Rashad stepped back and took in his surroundings, plenty of folks around. "Listen, your business is always welcome but not that punk ass Kyle. He owes me a lot of money."

John Robinson no longer wore his sunglasses, the sun having slowly diminished. "What about my daughter? Did she owe you some money?" His fists were clenched and spittle was coming from the side of his mouth.

"What you talking about?" Rashad asked with genuine honesty. He was baffled at the large man's hostility.

"It seems you and your ape of a cousin paid a visit to Kyle on Friday. Decided to take a pound of flesh from him. Now, can't say I fault you there.

Twerp had it coming I'm sure. Thing is, he had company that night… you know, Vicky… my daughter."

Rashad covered his mouth in a childlike gesture. "We was just trying to scare her man. Nothing happened! I swear. We didn't touch one strand of her blonde hair!"

John Robinson had been one second away from unleashing a brutal attack on the youth when his mind stuttered on the words. "Blonde hair?"

Rashad wasn't even aware of his luck as he carried on. "Derek and I just wanted to frighten Kyle. We were gonna use the girl as collateral. We never was gonna touch her or anything." He saw only confusion in the bald man's eyes. "This whole thing has been overblown dude. Tell Kyle he's good with us and accept my apology." He reached out to offer a handshake.

John Robinson gritted his teeth and reared back to land a deafening blow to Kyle's chin, but his punch never connected. Instead, he collapsed to the ground, a look of shock on his face.

It took Rashad a moment to comprehend what had happened. In front of him stood a young brother with a retro afro and a brick in his hand. The edge of the brick was soaked in the crimson blood of John Robinson. The man looked at Rashad in disgust.

"Don't stand there like you want to blow me. Help me get this cracker to his truck."

Rashad blinked twice and then snapped out of his shell shock. "Hell yeah! I thought I was gonna have to waste his ass right here in public." This last boast was more of a pipe dream. Rashad didn't carry a gun, and it was doubtful that John Robinson would have allowed him to get an advantage in a physical confrontation.

The newcomer said nothing. He grabbed the tow truck driver under the arms and instructed Rashad to grab the legs. Incredibly, none of the parents or ball players at the field seemed to notice or if they did, no interest was shown. In a matter of seconds, the two men had loaded John Robinson's limp form into the truck.

"I knew Derek would come through for me. I'll let him know you are one stand up brother."

The man said nothing. He simply stared at Rashad. "Well?"

"What you need bro? It's on the house. Weed, whatever, you name it."

For the first time the man showed some emotion. He smiled. "I need you to get away from the car… unless you'd like me to bust open your skull too?"

Rashad took the hint. He turned and walked away as quickly as possible. Out of the corner of his eye, he saw his savior pull out of the lot and head off calmly down Dorchester Avenue, the unconscious form of John Robinson forced to ride shotgun in his own truck. Rashad relocated his burner and tried Derek again.

"Why aren't you picking up?"

Jenna had spent an hour extracting the money from the paperbacks and had carefully wrapped rubber bands around five small stacks. These she had placed inside a DSW shoe box and placed it up in the cupboard. She'd think of a better place for it once she could concentrate, but her body was craving nourishment.

She marched down Salem Street and ordered a chicken cutlet sub from Monica's and brought it back to her apartment. In the five minutes she had gone, someone had left a message on her answering machine. She tapped a finger on the playback button.

"Hi Jenna. It's Martin. Just wanted to say hi. I called the Faulkner and they told me your friend Vicky is doing fine." There was a long pause on the message. "Chuck says hello or in his case ola. He'd like to see you again, and so would I."

A huge grin washed over her face. It was quickly replaced by a sense of remorse. *Here I am fawning over a policeman when I Just helped steal forty grand from a stranger in Salem.*

She looked down at her coffee table where she had placed the sergeant's business card. The blue BPD logo stood out prominently and added to her sense of guilt. In that moment, she decided she would confess the break-in to him, regardless of the consequences. If there was to be a future for them it could not start off with deception and lies. She erased the message and brought her sandwich over to the sofa. It was seven-thirty, time for some laughs with the zany characters of Big Bang Theory.

When John Robinson finally awoke the sun had tucked itself in for the evening. His head was throbbing; his skull felt like it was partially crushed in. He hadn't felt the attack but he knew someone must have been responsible for his predicament.

He tried to appraise his situation. He was in some sort of warehouse, apparently abandoned from the look of it. The floors and walls were bare, only layers of dust and rat turd occupied the space. The air itself was moldy and dry. He felt bile rise up in his lungs and it took a mighty effort to resist purging.

The door at the far end of the room opened a crack and two men entered, one carrying a lantern. It was the afro headed man who had knocked him out, along with another man. John Robinson stared at them both, recognizing neither man. He had no other reaction, not fear, nothing.

"What do you spear chuckers want from me?" he demanded.

Afro held the lantern close to the burly man's face. "You don't look so good man."

Robinson was tied to a metal folding chair with fishing line. "Let me up from this chair, and we'll find out how good I feel," he threatened. He struggled with the binds, but his circulation was cut off from sitting in the chair so long. His movement had no effect.

The other man was shorter and neatly dressed in a purple Perry Ellis button down and black Dockers. His flared nostrils and darkened skin suggested Haitian or Nigerian roots. Robinson couldn't tell. Nor did he care. *A spook is a spook.* He thought.

Purple shirt placed a firm hand on the big man's chin, his thumb scrapping against the soul patch. "I don't wish to spend my night talking to you." He circled Robinson and placed a hand on the wound at the back of his skull. "I don't think it's in your interest to be here all night either so let's get to the point. You took something from me and I want it back."

John Robinson snarled at the tiny man. "I don't have any idea what you're talking about. Never seen your ugly face before. Or maybe I did. Didn't I see you in the Planet of the Apes movie?"

Purple shirt said nothing. He simply nodded at Afro.

Robinson continued to push buttons. "Is this where your guy brains me again?"

In response, Afro brought out a pack of smokes. He lit one and puffed on it madly. He stared at his companion. "Now?"

The stout youth in purple and black simply nodded again. Without a word, Afro plunged the lit cigarette into John Robinson's exposed wound. He ground it there as hard as he could. "Arrogant cracker. Next one burns your dick."

Robinson fought back the pain. Every fiber in him begged to scream. Instead, he continued his umbrage. "Oh I bet you'd like that you fucking pillow biter. When I get out of this chair, I'm gonna…"

Afro didn't let him finish the statement. He unloaded an overhand right into the big man's face, crushing his nose and sending splatters of blood everywhere.

Purple shirt glared down at the flecks of blood that covered his pants. "Now look what you've done. All you had to do was give me the information. You have my money. I want it back. That's it man. Whole story."

"You got the wrong guy."

Afro swung again. This time he hooked a vicious left to the man's temple. The big driver almost went over, but his bulk kept the chair from tipping. Purple shirt took the lantern and held it against Robinson's face. "Stubborn man. You weren't that difficult to find. Nobody else has a logo with a black cat on their tow truck. My woman remembers it well."

John Robinson was dazed. He had lost a lot of blood, and was tired. He battled to stay awake knowing his life might depend on it. 'I'm listening." He croaked. "What did she say?"

Purple shirt relaxed a bit. He could see the burly man was weakened. Still, caution ruled as he backed away a step. "Said you were the one who claimed her car. Snatched it right out from under her."

"That's my job. I'm a repo man. I don't steal cars. You should have paid the fucking bill."

Afro lit another smoke. John Robinson braced himself for the oncoming blow, but nothing happened. Instead, the man placed the smoke up to his lips. "Cigarette?" Before the big man could answer, a hand shoved the lit smoke into his mouth. He spat it out immediately.

Purple shirt ignored the entire incident, went on as if it never happened. "Granted, Barbara is awful with her finances, but she gives the best head I've ever had so I forgive her shortcomings. Besides I never liked that Prius. It's a white man's car."

Robinson's ears perked up. He was a businessman first and foremost. His memory was always sharp when it came to business. "Winthrop Avenue in Revere? I picked up a 2014 Prius there a couple of weeks ago." A look of confusion shadowed his swollen features. "What does this have to do with money?"

Afro kicked him in the chest hard enough to topple the chair. "Quit fucking around man."

Purple shirt waved him off. "There was forty thousand dollars in that car. Barbara didn't know it was there. I had hidden it in the trunk."

"Bullshit!" John Robinson looked like a turtle on his back. He no longer seemed so menacing. "There wasn't anything but a bag of old clothes..."

Kyle! That fucking liar!

Afro drove a knee into his abdomen. He then pulled out an old fashioned switchblade. He loved retro style. "Now we getting somewhere."

Purple shirt crouched down and whispered to John Robinson. "Do you have any idea where we are?" He didn't wait for a response. "We are in historic Plymouth, birth place of the first batch of white thieves. They were very similar to you, sir. Using might against a minority. But I am not a Native American. No, I'm a proud black man so it's fitting that I choose this location to decide your fate."

"Let's talk it over," Robinson muttered.

He was cut off. "See those early white men once had a thriving business here. Largest producers of rope in the country at one point. That's where we are now. In Cordage Park. Inside one of the abandoned warehouses conveniently located near the train tracks." He rocked the lantern back and forth in front of the giant. "I'm thinking of throwing your body on those tracks. Train will mash you up real good." He let out a hearty laugh. "And don't fall for that CSI bullshit. The police will chalk you up as another white man who couldn't cope with his failed business."

"I don't have the money."

"Course not. Let's not waste any more time. Let's drop this fool on the tracks in time for the final run."

Robinson flailed against his restraints. "Wait! I said I don't have it. Didn't say I didn't know where it is."

Purple shirt grinned madly. "You have my full attention."

In the heat of desperation, John Robinson sang like a canary. He sacrificed Kyle without a moment's hesitation. Of course it would all be in vain. Afro and Purple shirt briefly debated the trucker's fate, but in the end, one comment had sealed Robinson's fate.

Afro placed a shoe on the brawny man's neck. "Planet of the apes? Seriously?"

Jenna awoke to the buzzing of her cell phone. She had been in a deep sleep, dreaming of a gigantic amusement park. She rubbed her eyes and focused on the digital clock. It had been a house warming gift from her mom. 7:52 am!

"Hello?" she asked in a nervous tone.

She didn't recognize the voice at first. It was Vicky. "Jenna? Hi, it's

Vicky. Sorry for calling so early in the morning, but it's the only time there isn't a line for the house phone."

"Don't worry about it. How are you feeling?"

Vicky didn't respond immediately. It was as if she were weighing her words. "Ashamed, afraid, you name it. I have this really odd sensation this morning and I can't place a finger on it." She paused. "But that's not why I'm calling."

"What do I owe the pleasure for?" asked Jenna.

"First of all, thank your boyfriend for me. He sent over some fresh clothes last night with the tags still on them. Not garbage either, I'm talking nice stuff."

Jenna couldn't help herself. "He's not my boyfriend." She blurted out.

"Sorry, I just assumed you and Sarge were an item. He couldn't stop talking about you last night."

Jenna brightened at the news. "And second of all?"

"That's just it. He arranged for me to get out of this place. Some treatment center in Brookline. The nurses here told me he must have pulled some strings to get me a bed."

"That's wonderful news Vicky. When are you going?"

"That's just it. I need a ride. Do you think your Spanish friends could help?"

Jenna stifled a laugh. An image of Edna hurling a frying pan flashed by her eyes. "Probably not a good idea right now. I'll try and reach Marty and see if he can help out. I'll give you a call as soon as I hear back from him."

"Thanks, Jenna. You have been like a guardian angel to me. I know that sounds corny, but I never had any siblings or even friends, just Kyle. And you know how that turned out."

Jenna ignored the compliment. "Have you tried contacting him?"

"No way. He'd tell Daddy I was in trouble, and that bastard would make things ten times worse." Her voice had begun to crack. "That's been my father's answer to problems my entire life. He'd just blame me and magnify my role in it. If it wasn't for him, I would never have met Kyle."

Jenna feared any further comment on the situation could only be negative. She changed the subject as quickly as possible. "Let me down some coffee and figure out a way to get you out of there. In the meantime, stay strong sweetie. There are people who care about you."

She hung up and dialed Sergeant Conrad.

«—»

Martin Conrad was able to procure an early lunch break. He had expected the call from Jenna and was relieved to hear that his behind the scenes manipulation had resulted in securing a bed for Vicky. He pulled up in his own car, Jenna already waiting out front.

She had used the brief hours in between to dash over to Grant Maxell's shop for a bouquet of mixed flowers. Naturally, he had declined her offer to pay. Much to his chagrin, she had left a twenty dollar bill on the counter and scooted out before he could protest. She had shouted out a promise of a coffee date while heading back toward her apartment.

After a brief shower, she had chosen a conservative blue dress from her closet. She hoped to catch Martin Conrad's eye, but at the same time she felt the need to express a sense of professionalism. It dawned on her that she was no longer a fraternity girl, but had blossomed into a member of the working class.

The Sergeant took note of her appearance. If he was impressed, he didn't betray it. Instead he put on an air of business and proceeded to make small talk the entire way to the Faulkner. Jenna was slightly disappointed, but dismissed it. He was in uniform, and she took that as a sign that duty would take precedent over desire.

She resigned herself to the fact that today would be about Vicky's well being and nothing more.

When the pair reached the hospital, they spent a few moments with Vicky's doctor going over details. Jenna was horrified to learn that Vicky had track marks between her toes, a common method of deception used by many junkies. The good news was that her blood had been tested and found free of hepatitis or any other disease common among drug users.

"She's fortunate to have you folks backing her cause," the doctor said. "With some guidance and better judgement, she can lick this habit. It's in her hands now."

Martin and Jenna thanked the doctor and rushed in to see Vicky. She was dressed in a pink two piece cotton pajama set that made her look even younger than her years. Jenna marveled at the transformation. Just days ago, this tiny girl had looked like a tired old hag. Now she was filled with vigor.

"My favorite Disney couple!" Vicky proclaimed. She gave Jenna an exaggerated wink that said you-can't-fool-me! "Come to rescue me?"

Jenna noticed she still clutched the Belle pillow in her arms. "Well of course. How else would I get that back?" She snapped her fingers. "Hand it over, girl."

Vicky smiled and clutched the pillow, genuine warmth emanating from her. "Only if you give me visitation rights?"

The trio laughed and shared small talk. Jenna and Martin packed a duffel bag while Vicky padded off to the bathroom to get changed. Everything was going according to plan, when the floor fell out from underneath them in the form of two uniformed police officers.

Martin Conrad ushered them into the hallway and the three men exchanged brief comments. When Marty returned Jenna could see the look of dismay on his face. Jenna felt her heart sink. "Now what?"

At that moment Vicky emerged from the bathroom, dressed neatly in a pair of jeans and a Boston Strong t-shirt. Her eyes darted back and forth from the three cops to Jenna.

"Oh no!" She whispered. "Something happened to Kyle."

Martin Conrad came over and placed his hands on her shoulders. "Vicky, we need to talk about your father."

The turmoil that followed the announcement of John Robinson's suicide sent Jenna's day spinning into a tizzy. She deferred all decisions to Martin Conrad and the doctors of the Faulkner Hospital. In the end, it was concluded that it would be in the best interest of everyone that Vicky remain at the facility for another day, her transfer pushed back until tomorrow.

Jenna had wanted to stay and comfort the young girl, but she was urged to leave. Vicky's fragile state of mind was in a dangerous flux, and so her doctor decided to sedate her. The dwarfish girl was hysterical. Her last words before drifting off would haunt Jenna for some time to come.

"Daddy killed himself because of me! I was nothing but a disappointment."

The words continued to echo in her ears as she rode in silence with Martin Conrad. Any thoughts of revealing the contents of the shoebox to the police sergeant were now shelved indefinitely. Jenna felt it best to just keep it to herself. John Robinson no longer posed a threat to his daughter. Thus the money could be handed over to Vicky. She'd need it for the upkeep of her home and a chance to start a new life.

Convinced this was the rightful conclusion to the saga, Jenna settled back and let her mind focus on other matters, mainly the handsome man behind the wheel. Throughout the entire incident, Martin had kept his composure, his police training and experience helping to ease both girls from the shock of the news. Jenna wondered how many times he had broken the news to loved ones about their family. Her thoughts drifted back to the story of Marty's own father, Ross, and how his partner and best friend Joe had the unenviable task of delivering the heart breaking news to a young widow.

"Thanks for being there today." They were parked outside her apartment, the engine idling. Martin had called his Captain and explained the situation, careful to mention the other officers involved. The Captain was a compassionate man and had told him to take the rest of the day off and just write it up as part of his daily log. Martin had thanked the man, and Jenna suspected there might be a connection between the two. Sheepishly, Martin revealed that his Captain had served with his father many moons ago. There was a lot of nepotism in the police department and bonds were constantly established. Further prodding, revealed the man to be his godfather.

Martin Conrad circled the street twice before hawking out a spot. He squeezed his SUV into it, slipped his police placard from the visor to the dashboard, and escorted Jenna from the vehicle.

He stared past her black frame glasses, into her blues eyes. "Don't take this the wrong way, but your misfortune keeps turning into my good luck. "He allowed his eyes to soak in her outfit. "Did I mention how beautiful you look?"

"Why sergeant I didn't think you had noticed? "

The brawny man shrugged, his freckles contrasting with his sinewy neck. "I'm trained to notice these things Ms. Coyne. "

"What else have you noticed?"

"Lots of things," he considered. "You don't own a car. That tells me you're a creature of habit, content in your surroundings. "

Jenna conceded. "Go on."

"You live alone, no roommates. Tells me you do well enough at your job."

She laughed. "I may be quitting that job." She didn't bother to elaborate. "Why so inquisitive, Sherlock?"

Martin Conrad grasped her in his arms and kissed her. "Because I've fallen for you."

Secretly, Jenna had hoped to recreate the passion of their previous encounter, but the events of the day and the sorrow over Vicky's loss, had cast a somber mood on the evening.

Martin Conrad had suggested a quiet evening of takeout back at his apartment. He later confessed it was Chuck's idea.

"Little guy really took a liking to you." He commented. He had removed his shirt and stood before her in an immaculate wife beater.

Jenna's eyes focused on a nasty bruise above the big man's breast and a second one underneath his shoulder blade. He caught her concern. "Just a scratch. Took a spill chasing a perp."

She doubted his story. "Wasn't there the other night."

Sensing Jenna's concern, Martin Conrad grabbed two bottles of Miller Lite from his fridge and plopped down on the sofa. He popped off the cap and handed her one. "Jenna, let's talk about the elephant in the room. " He twisted off the other cap and took a long swig from the neck. "I'm a cop. It's a dangerous job." He gulped down another long swig, almost finishing the contents. "Cops and love don't mix well. It is what it is."

She pondered his words, images of the events of the last few days drifting in and out her mind. She put down the bottle, feeling queasy.

Marty continued. "There will be a lot of sleepless nights and you will learn to hate the phone and the doorbell. You will stop watching the news." He went into the kitchen and got another beer. "Should I continue or are you seeing a pattern?"

Jenna sought comfort in the form of the Jack Russell. He nuzzled up against her leg and she reached down and stroked him behind the ears. "You're trying to scare me?"

"No, Jenna. I'm trying to prepare you." He sat back down on the sofa. "I have to make sure you understand the situation."

Jenna joined him on the sofa. She sought to lighten the mood. Her fingers brushed lightly over the yellow bruise. "I got a paper cut at work last week."

The burly man took her in his arms. "Care to show me?" His fingers wrestled with the zipper on the back of her dress.

She kissed him gently. "Shouldn't you read me my rights first?"

Jenna awoke to the smell of coffee and the sounds of television, more specifically an early morning variety show on one of the Latin networks. Chuck was curled up on the coffee table, apparently enthralled with the broadcast. "Where is your roomie?"she called out to the dog.

The jack Russell gave no hint of acknowledgement.

"Fine, be anti-social." Jenna mocked. She twisted over and saw the note on the night table. She picked it up and perused through the brief message.

"At work. Cab money on fridge. Miss you."

She frowned, remembering Marty's impassioned speech last night. "Good morning to you too."

Gathering up her clothing she headed into the bathroom. She stopped to pat Chuck, but his eyes remained glued on the small flat screen. Some heavy set man was juggling bowling pins, while surrounded by scantily clad girls, all blowing on party trumpets. "Must be contagious," she muttered at the dog. He continued to ignore her.

A half hour later she was back in the North End, making a brief stop at the White Hen Pantry for some Mountain Dew Code Red.

"Gina, my most precious flower!" It was Grant Maxwell, playing his morning lottery before work. He observed her for a moment. If he noticed she wore the same clothes from yesterday, he was too much of a gentleman to say anything.

Jenna grabbed two bottles of the popular soda. "Good morning."

"Yes, it is," he responded, indifferently. "How did your friend like the flowers?"

Jenna sighed. "Unfortunately, I might need to order some more. " She saw his curiosity was peaked.

She proceeded to tell him about the suicide of Vicky's father. The elderly man listened attentively, not venturing any opinions nor suggestions. He offered to walk her home and she graciously accepted. It was another muggy day, and she couldn't wait to get out of her dress and into something more comfortable. The pair chatted amiably all the way to Prince Street.

Neither one of them noticed anything odd about the tall black man on the corner, sporting an afro, and barking animatedly into his cell phone.

Wednesday ...hump day. Jenna hadn't worked in days, but she still felt the drain. She had spent an hour on the internet searching for jobs in her field. They were few and far between, especially in the Boston area where liberal arts degrees were handed out like Christmas gifts.

Her boredom had led her to reach out to Marta in hopes of hooking up for dinner. Her young friend declined at first, using her early morning work shift as an excuse, but when Jenna had agreed to meet her in East

Boston, Marta finally relented and accepted the offer.

They both agreed on Santarpios over near Airport Station. It was a well known landmark in the New England area, and even though Marta wasn't too crazy about the pizza itself, she did crave the house wine.

"Why can't Ma and I make our wine taste like this?" she demanded. She had ordered a carafe of the fabulous elixir, knowing full well that she planned on asking for a refill.

Jenna sipped at her own glass appreciatively. She had dressed in simple white capris, and a black and white checkered top. "If you can master this recipe, I'll become an alcoholic."

They updated each other on the events of the past couple of days.

"I'm sorry to hear about that girl's dad, but I'm not surprised. She seemed like a troll, and that lazy boyfriend. What a jerk!" Marta had begun to slur, even though she hadn't quite finished her second glass.

Jenna remained neutral. "I'm just glad Marty helped her out. "

The waiter came over and dropped off an order of lamb. It came on a tray with hot stemmed peppers and warm bread. Marta helped herself to the bread immediately. "I can't let Ma see me having bread. She keeps torturing me about my weight."

As if on que, Edna Ruiz marched into the restaurant. You could have played Darth Vader's imperial theme music. The eternally young mother had come directly from work. Dressed in her concierge outfit, which consisted of a crisp white blouse, blue vest and bowtie, and a knee length skirt over hosiery, she was the picture of modesty. A far cry from her usual style. Even her hair, which was usually poofed out with hairspray and modeled after 1980's music videos, remained somber in a tight bun. Everything about her screamed military.

Marta refilled her glass and slugged back a greedy gulp. "Mami! You made it." The accent was unmistakable.

Edna frowned. "I hope you have saved up a personnel day? Because I smell a hangover coming." She reached over and kissed Jenna on the cheek. "And you, don't get use to this lazy lifestyle."

Jenna giggled and called over the waiter. She flashed the empty carafe at him, and he nodded affirmatively. "You look wonderful Edna."

"Please," the woman began. "Between this damn tie and these freaking pantyhose, I can't breathe. "

Marta snorted her disapproval. "Don't worry Mami. When we get home you can let it all hang out."

Edna dismissed her. "That's just it baby. My stuff doesn't hang, cause

I take care of myself. Why can't you join the gym? It's covered in your insurance plan."

Jenna snatched a piece of bread, hoping to make Marta feel more comfortable. "Any job openings Edna?"

Turning her attention away from her daughter's weight, Edna focused on Jenna. "Baby, the hotel business is dying like everything else. The days of traveling salesmen and business conventions are over. Everyone uses the internet for meetings now. You don't even have to leave your house. The only openings we have right now are in housekeeping and in the kitchen, because there will always be no shortage of lazy bastards who don't want to cook or clean."

The waiter dropped off a fresh carafe of the dark wine. Marta snagged it and filled her cup in one splash. "Ladies and gentlemen, that message brought to you by mother, Miss Perfect." She drained the glass in one gulp. "Yes, I said Miss. Like everyone else in East Boston, she's an unmarried mother." She stood up and waved her glass. "Don't let the outfit fool you either. Catch her on weekends when the goods are on display."

Jenna tugged at her friend's arm. "Stop it Marta, that's your mother!"

The girl ignored her. She reached for the carafe, but Jenna was faster. Marta frowned. "You too Jennie? Little miss perfect, blonde and blue eyed and riding Prince Charming."

Jenna started to respond, but Marta wouldn't cease her rant. "For four years I heard my mother's nagging voice. Why can't you act like her? Why can't you dress like her, look like her? Beautiful little Jennie. Skinny Jennie. Why Mami? Why do you do this to me?"

Edna was startled. She sought Jenna's eyes. *Help me*. She almost said it out loud.

"I go to work every day in that crappy building," Marta had begun to sob. "I'm tired Mami. I'm tired of walking home and seeing all the boys drool over you and Jennie. I'm tired of it." She wiped a tear from her eyes. "I'm twenty-one years old. When is someone going to notice me?"

Marta turned on her heels and exited Santarpios. Jenna started to go after her, but a firm hand from Edna stopped her. "Give her some space."

Jenna did as instructed. Her hands were trembling.

"Sorry you saw that," commented Edna. She poured Jenna a refill and helped herself to a glass. "I knew this was coming."

Jenna was confused. "She's always been quiet and shy, but never so angry."

The waiter brought them a large cheese pizza. Edna took a slice and bit

"Baby, the hotel business is dying..."

into it. It was delicious, but her mood dampened the enjoyment.

"I guess it's me. I smother her, I admit it, but it's only because I love her so much." She washed down a mouthful with the wine. "Do you think it's unhealthy for a mother to hang out with her daughter?"

Jenna pondered the question. She thought of her own mom, plagued by arthritis and forced to walk with a cane. "No, Edna, I don't."

"How can I fix this? How can I make my baby feel better?"

Jenna concentrated. "How do you cope with your stressful day Edna?" She didn't wait for the answer. "You come home like Clark Kent. You can't wait to get out of that office garb and put on your flashy cape and costume!"

"Madre de dios!" Edna blurted out. "I follow you. She deserves what every girl wants."

They stared at each other, grinning madly, and then both uttered the word at the same time.

"Makeover!"

That night, sitting cross legged on her sofa, scrapping at a Luigi's Italian Ice, cherry flavor, naturally, Jenna was the picture of content.

"God that's good!"

The crisis with the Ruiz had passed. Turned out, Marta was only outside; puffing on a cigarette and watching cars enter the Callahan Tunnel. Her state of intoxication had probably been exaggerated as a means to vent her frustrations, and when alerted to the suggestion of a self-indulged pampering session, she had accepted the news with glee. Jenna had left the pair, confident that any issues would be resolved.

She put down her frosty spoon and snatched up her cell phone. Time to check in with Vicky. She kept her fingers crossed tightly, as the floor monitor went to seek the troubled youngster.

"Hello?" Vicky questioned.

"Hi, it's me Jenna. Just checking to see how you are doing?"

"Fine. This place is nice, but the other patients are so gloomy." She paused, reflecting. "I can only imagine how obnoxious I must have been."

Jenna cut her short. "The important thing is that you acknowledged your problem. That took courage. You're a lot stronger than you think."

"Thanks, Jenna. I keep thinking of my father. In some ways, he was a lot like me. He was hurting, and he couldn't bring himself to ask for help. "

"Vicky ..."

"No, Jenna. Let me finish. You're probably wondering how I could let someone do the things he did to me? Well, you weren't the first you know. I could go through a list of teachers, doctors, even Grandpa. I mean, daddy didn't exactly cover his trail, but I always blamed myself."

Jenna couldn't help but ask "Why?"

"Not for making him hit me. I blamed myself for not helping him. He lost his wife and I was all he had. I should have stepped up."

"No, Vicky. He was a parent. He should have refocused his energy on taking care of you. He had an obligation to you. And he owed it to your mom to try."

Vicky was sobbing. "I think he did try Jenna. I really do. There were times he was so nice."

"Those are the memories you should carry with you honey. He's at peace now, and you will come to take comfort in that once your grief fades."

Vicky nodded. 'Thanks Jenna. You always know what to say. I think my time is up."

"Ok, stay out of trouble," Jenna advised.

"But how will I see handsome Sarge?"

"Hands off girl," Jenna kidded. "That one is mine."

"You deserve it. Goodnight Jenna."

"Goodnight, honey."

Jenna disconnected from her call and resumed picking at the Italian ice. The sun still set early in June and with it came a much needed respite from the humidity. She opened her second floor window to allow the breeze to enter. The neighborhood was quiet, a far cry from next month, when the weekly feasts would begin.

She turned on the early news and settled back on the sofa. The local news was rehashing the events of the day while a scrolling ticker at the bottom of the screen filled the viewer in on breaking news. She wasn't really paying mind when out of the corner of her eye she saw the headline:

Police Cruiser involved in two car crash near south Station.

Instantly, her heart skipped a beat, an image of handsome Martin Conrad exploded into her mind. "Oh my God, he was right!" she muttered out loud. She immediately pressed the Netflix button on her remote. A minute later, an old episode of Ghost Whisperer was streaming onto her screen.

She wanted to call him so badly, yet she resisted.

Is it too much, too fast?

She really couldn't be sure. There had been boyfriends in the past. Physical needs had been met. But this felt different. Felt right. She even dared to conjure up thoughts of the dreaded "L" word.

Her eyes wandered around the apartment. There were the usual mom and pop photos, not to mention a really cute photo of herself with Vicky and Edna standing on the deck of the luxury liner, the Odyssey. Fortunately, they snap those as you board the cruise ship because by the end of the voyage they all had been tipsy. There were also some photos from her college days, but that was it.

Mom and Dad had always showered her with beautiful gifts, but vacations had been far and few, the plight of many children born to older parents these days. She thought back to earlier in the evening when Marta had been delivering her woe-is-me soliloquy. Crazy girl didn't know how lucky she was to have such a young mom who could also double as a playmate. Must have been fun practicing dance moves when your mom was in her prime and could teach you everything.

Her phone was vibrating. She scooped it up quickly and read the text.

"Miss you." It was from Martin Conrad.

A wave of euphoria shot up and down her body. She typed furiously. "Ditto. You were right. LOL."

She waited a few minutes to see if the online bantering would continue, but when it didn't she resigned herself to call it a night. The wine from Santarpios had combined with the heat to make her dehydrated and tired. She didn't even bother to pull down the bedspread. She just curled up in the fetal position and drifted off to slumberland.

She was unaware of the activity taking place in the apartment across the hall.

Kyle could not believe his good fortune as he entered his apartment on Prince Street. Even the sight of his own blood stains on the floor could not deter his uplifted spirits. He felt like opening the window and screaming to the top of his lungs.

"Robinson is dead?"

It repeated over and over in his mind. The news had come as a shock after discovering his money had been pilfered. With no place to go and in need of a pick me up, he had spent the night in John Robinson's decrepit Salem home. He knew the big man liked his marijuana, and sure enough a short search had scored up a few joints. Kyle had puffed away contently when company had arrived in the form of Vicky's Aunt June. Fortunately, the woman had remembered Kyle from a previous holiday outing, and was not taken aback by his presence.

With teary eyes, the woman informed Kyle of his employer's suicide at the rail road station in Plymouth. Kyle had been genuinely shocked. John Robinson was not the type to take his own life. If anything, his entire mission in life appeared to be the torture and humiliation of others. This group spared no one, family, customers, and most of all Kyle.

But then came the frosting on the cake. Auntie June spilled the beans that Vicky had been holed up in the detox unit at the Faulkner hospital, and after having been informed of her father's untimely demise, had been sent over to a different rehab unit in Brookline.

All of this news hit Kyle like a sledgehammer, but Christmas wasn't over yet. Nope, the gifts kept coming. When Aunt June went over to inform the neighbors, pothead Kyle had tagged along for some fresh air, and much to his disbelief found out that Vicky, some blonde, and two Spanish girls had visited the house on Sunday, departing with a box from the garage.

"Bingo!"

The mystery had been solved. The apple hadn't fallen far from the tree. Vicky had proven to be as adept at skullduggery as her old man.

Reflecting on his good fortune, he surveyed his apartment. The damage was not too bad. A broken chair and a puddle of blood on the carpets. Rashad and Derek had been foiled in their attempt to teach him a lesson by some crazy Latino chick with a swing like Big Papi.

"Spanish girls and a blonde? Could it be?"

Blaming his paranoia on the weed, he shrugged off the idea and went over to the fridge. He never cooked for himself, but Vicky always insisted on having food on hand for the inevitable munchies that followed his pot binging. He found some salami still in the wrapper, sniffed it twice with caution, and then scoffed it anyway.

First order of business, to pleasure himself followed by a good night's rest and then tomorrow he would make a visit to Brookline in a quest to regain his money. He knew it would only be a matter of time before Derek and Rashad came knocking again. In fact he had given himself quite a scare when he first turned the corner on his street and had spotted a black man, a rare sight in this neighborhood, but thankfully it had just been some dude with a big afro smiling while he took bites from one of the local vendor's sausages.

«—»

Thursday morning brought some much needed relief from the torrid weather that had been sweltering for the past few days. It also brought with it a down pour in the form of buckets of rain. The force of the pattering on her windows woke Jenna from a blissful sleep. She started to reach for the remote to check out the weather forecast, but remembered her scare from last night's broadcast so she just checked her laptop instead.

Accuweather predicted an early ending for the rainfall, so she decided to plan on a day out. She showered and changed into fresh clothing and sipped coffee from the Keurig.

"How can people sit home all day?" she wondered.

It was eight in the morning and all she could think of was dreamy Sergeant Conrad. Unable to resist the urge, she texted him. "Good morning."

She was startled when the cell rang.

"Good morning to you too." His voice was muffled by sounds in the background. "I'm at the precinct so it might get noisy."

"I miss you." She felt foolish as soon as she said it. What am I thirteen? "I know I sound like a nut."

The big man had an affectionate laugh. "Not at all. I was thinking the same thing. I have a busy day but tomorrow night I'm free."

Jenna brightened slightly. "I know but I'm so bored and I can't believe I'm saying this but I miss work too."

"Now you know why I have a roommate," he paused. "You know, Chuck is house trained. You are more than welcome to borrow him."

"I might take you up on that offer."

"Good. There is a spare key taped underneath the metal railing. I know, me of all people, shouldn't have one but I can't tell you how many times I've been dropped off without my keys and I just got tired of having to head back to the station." There was a long pause. "In fact, I've been thinking."

Jenna interrupted. "I bet I would smell wood burning," she joked. She had an insight into what may be coming next.

"Why don't you keep the key Jenna?"

Her heart skipped a beat. "I'd like that. Besides, all these years with Marta, I've picked up quite an ear for Spanish, so I think me and Chuck will get along fine."

"Great. Gotta run."

She waited to make sure he had hung up before whispering "I love you."

«—»

The internet website had correctly predicted the weather. By ten a.m. the rain had cleared up and the sun emerged but without much of the sweltering heat it had been dealing out recently. Jenna was delighted with the temperature shift and elected to take the MBTA ferry from Aquarium over to the Charlestown Navy Yard. There she spent a half hour admiring Old Ironsides before heading over to Martin Conrad's apartment to retrieve Chuck.

Surprisingly, the rambunctious animal gave her no difficulties with the leash. In moments, the unlikely pair were on their way back home. She decided to really put the dog to the test by walking back home. Again, the Jack Russell amazed her by complying with her wish. He trekked over the bridge like a show dog, soaking in the atmosphere. She couldn't have been more pleased.

And then they reached Commercial Street. Chuck began to growl urgently, and Jenna spun around to see a familiar face.

"Kyle!" She blurted, taken aback by the young man. His face still showed evidence of the brutal beating he had endured in her presence.

"Listen, I know we never really talked before, but I owe you an apology and a thank you. Your bat swinging friend saved my life," he offered.

Jenna gripped the leash on Chuck. She had no idea of the dog's background, and the last thing she wanted was for it to be involved in an incident. She said nothing to Kyle, waiting to see what he wanted.

"I guess you know I owed those guys some cash, and they mistook you for a friend of mine, actually my girlfriend, Vicky." He searched her eyes for recognition, but Jenna held sway, feigning ignorance. "You probably have seen her a dozen times come to visit me?"

"What is it you want? " Jenna gritted out impatiently.

Kyle raised his hands in defense. "Whoa! Easy. It's like I said, I just wanted to tell you I was sorry and to thank your friend for saving us. I forgot her name. What was it again?"

Jenna didn't take the bait. "The police are still looking for the men who did this to you."

"So am I." Kyle boasted. "Oh don't worry it's not like that at all. I just want to pay off my debt. You see I recently came into some money. " He again held eye contact with her, his face becoming stern. "Although I misplaced it."

"I hope you find it." She whispered with uncertainty.

A malicious grin formed on the young man's face. "Oh I will. See, I didn't exactly lose it. It was stolen from me, but I know who took it. It's just a matter of time before I find out where it is."

Jenna felt her hands tremble and she let go of the leash. Chuck bared all his teeth at Kyle, letting him know his presence was not going to be tolerated further. "It's ok, Chuck." She stepped on the thin leash in order to pick it up. "We're leaving now."

"Please remember to thank your friend for me," he urged. "And the other Spanish girl too. Hopefully, I'll be able to thank them in person soon."

Jenna turned and walked on. Her mind was reeling.

How could he know about Marta? She had remained downstairs during the attack. And those cryptic words about recovering the money? What could he know?

She reached down and hugged Chuck. "I hope your master taught you to be a watch dog?"

The rest of the afternoon was spent in a futile attempt to introduce Chuck to his new surroundings. He had refused to go up the staircase, insisting on being carried into the apartment. Once there, he mutated into a cat, darting from room to room, refusing to sit still. Fortunately, she was able to locate a Spanish soap opera on Hulu that caught his attention. Chuck couldn't locate a coffee table so he improvised with a kitchen chair, removing the chair pad she had just purchased from Target, unfortunately destroying the drawstrings in the process. Jenna was too tired to protest. She allowed the dog to have his way.

She wanted to call Marta and tell her about Kyle, but decided against it. Why scare the young girl? Forget about even telling Edna about the incident. She would be in her car in a second, barreling through the tunnel on a crazed blood thirst. No, the Ruiz's would have to remain oblivious to the situation.

What about Martin Conrad? Surely, she could confide in her shining knight? But she hadn't even told him about the forty thousand dollars. She had thought it belonged to John Robinson, making Vicky the rightful heir. But Kyle had seemed confident that he had been robbed of the cash. She doubted very much that he had come by it legally, but the fact still made her an accomplice to a theft, and the furthest thing from her mind was to involve Martin Conrad or the Boston Police Department in the matter. If push came to shove, she would return the money to Kyle. Maybe he would move out or spent it on drugs and overdose? She was immediately ashamed at her thoughts. He was probably not evil. Like Vicky, there was always a chance for reform. No one ever sets out to be a junkie or a criminal.

Turning her attention away from her troubles, and from her visitor, she watered the plants she had bought from Grant Maxwell, and opened up her windows to allow the cooler air to circulate. Prince Street was abuzz with foot traffic, a byproduct of the lunch hour crowd. Her eyes focused on Kyle down below, engaged in an animated conversation with a young black man, dressed rather garishly in a tan corduroy suit despite the summer weather. He looked like a refugee from a rerun of Starsky and Hutch, right down to the exaggerated 1970's afro.

Right back to drug dealing, Kyle? You deserve what you get.

She turned back to Chuck, asking him if he wanted to eat. Had she kept her attention focused on her neighbor just a moment longer, she would have seen the large man flash a blade at Kyle and order him into a car.

Vicky Sue Robinson was antsy. She sat in a scuffed recliner nestled in a corner of the rec room at the Woodburne Clinic. She had brought her Belle pillow along with her for the encounter. The ragged item had become her security blanket, a remembrance of better times. Times before Kyle, before John Robinson's descent into madness, and before the untimely death of her mother which had kick started this dark period of her life.

Her head throbbed, a side effect of the meds the doctors had forced on her to starve off the cravings for heroin. She felt like sleeping, but the on call nurse had alerted her that a visitor was on his way.

Probably Sarge.

The burly policeman had arranged the entire setup, along with dropping off fresh clothes and bathroom supplies. He was the first law enforcement person she had ever liked.

Lucky, Jenna.

She was taken aback when her boyfriend Kyle entered the room.

"Vicky! Thank god you are alright." He raced over and kissed her on the forehead.

Her pale skin seemed to drain further after taking in his appearance. "Oh, my god. I heard you were attacked at the apartment, but they didn't say it was this bad."

"It's nothing." He plunked himself down on the edge of the recliner.

"The important thing is that you're ok. I thought maybe Derek and Rashad had found you."

"They thought your neighbor was me."

Kyle let a moment pass, and then began rubbing her back. "She was in the wrong place at the wrong time." He grabbed hold of the stuffed pillow. "She probably told you about it."

"No, we haven't spoken."

Kyle searched her face. "Is that so? "

Vicky hesitated. "I don't know, maybe. I was pretty screwed up. I couldn't get back in the apartment, and she must have called an ambulance or something. I really can't remember."

"Not important. Anyway, I'm here because I heard about Big John. Real bummer. Never figured him for that in a million years. "

Tears welled up in Vicky's eyes. "Daddy, really liked you Kyle. He said you were a good guy, someone he could trust."

"Funny you say that. See, I never could trust your old man. He'd make promises to me and then break them. "

"Please don't talk about the dead."

"Let me finish. " He grabbed her hand. "I liked John. Man, I can't think of anyone I'd rather have at my side in a scrap, but that's as far as it goes. I knew John like a book. He came first, not me, not you. Just himself. Especially when it came to money."

Vicky rubbed her eyes. She knew Kyle too well. He was up to something. "Kyle, my father killed himself and I'm in here battling every urge to go out and get fried again, so stop pussyfooting around. What are you driving at?"

The youth giggled. "I could never fool you, could I? Vicky, all I ever wanted was for us to do better. That's why I didn't take John up on his offer to move in with you in Salem. Do you think I'm stupid?

He grew angry. "I knew what was going on. What he was doing to you. But I couldn't stop it. I was ashamed. I was afraid. You were my girl and I couldn't standup to the man. Even worse, I worked for him, pretending like everything was fine. That's why I turned to the hard stuff. It numbed me from his evil, and I thought it would work for you too.

"Vicky, I was keeping a secret from you and your father. I had saved up some money so we could run away; maybe go to Maine or New Hampshire. But I knew if Big John even sniffed at the plan, he'd put an end to it right away."

"Kyle…" she tried to interject.

"No," he continued. "So I decided to hide it. I knew my place was too dangerous. Too many people know I deal, and that made it an obvious target. So I turned my eyes toward Elm Street. I knew if I ever left it inside the house, one of you would find it. So, I hid it in the one place no Robinson would touch."

"The garage."

"Bingo. Your mother's shrine. Christ, for the longest time I actually thought it was a tomb and that the old man had buried her there. So I hid the money in the trunk, and I was going to surprise you the very same night Shad and Derek busted in."

Vicky wiped her mouth. A film of white froth was on her lips. She would need more meds soon. "Kyle, I want to believe you so badly…"

"It's true. I had enough there for us to get a trailer or something. But it's gone now. Taken right out of your mom's car." He kissed her on the lips gently. "I know it was you."

"Please, Kyle …"

He stood up and walked over to the window. "I forgive you. It was going to be your money, our money anyway." He motioned for her to join him at the window. " Doesn't make a difference now."

Vicky rose out of the recliner, a little unsteady on her feet and trudged over to the window. Kyle hugged her ferociously.

"See that dude over there? The Black guy with the funky hairdo? "He waited for her to nod. "That guy drove me here. It seems the money belongs to him."

"What?"

"It was in a car that Big John and I towed out of Revere. Just found out it belongs to that guy and his friends. Told me I have until tonight to return it or they kill me."

Vicky's eyes widened. "I don't believe you!"

"Like I said, it doesn't matter. I just wanted you to know what my intentions were."

"I …Kyle…"

He kissed her again. "I'm sorry about Big John, but at least he can't hurt you no more. With him gone, we could have turned everything around. Could have stayed in Salem, paid the bills, maybe slap some paint on the place, grow some flowers, that kind of stuff. No more drugs, booze." He hugged her again. "No more pain."

"Can't we call the police. I know someone…"

"Vicky, you know these guys. They won't stop until they get their money back. Just know that I love you, always have."

She held him fiercely. "Please Kyle, there has to be something we can do. You were right I did take the money."

"I know. The neighbors saw you and three other girls. It was the blonde from across the hall?"

"Her name is Jenna."

Afro saw Kyle through the window. He ran a finger across his throat. Time's up.

"Vicky, it doesn't matter now. If I don't return the money I'm dead." He graced a fingertip across her trembling lips. "Don't make me beg you for help."

The young girl's mind was reeling. She felt herself relapsing, and seeing Kyle this helpless and defeated wasn't improving her condition.

"You have to promise me," she barked. "Promise me no one gets hurt."

Kyle kissed her again. "Anything. Just help me."

She gulped. "Jenna has it. Back at Prince Street. It's in her apartment." She turned and buried her sobs into the Belle pillow.

"Thank you baby. When this is over, I'll come and get you. I promise this time it's for real."

She hugged him. "I love you Kyle. I'm sorry I did this to you."

"I know baby. I know you didn't mean to hurt me."

He turned and departed. Vicky ran to the window. She could see Afro standing in front of his car. He was scrapping under his fingernails with a shiny blade. It gave her the shivers.

What have I done?

She ran out of the rec room in search of a phone.

Jenna gripped her cell phone as tightly as possible. She had just ended a conversation with Vicky. Conversation wasn't the best description she could conjure up. She really couldn't think of any proper way to explain what she had heard. The phone call had been surreal. Vicky was babbling incoherently, stopping every so often to apologize, but two words came across loud and clear.

Kyle knows!

Chuck was yipping wildly, as if the pet sensed the urgency of the matter.

"Don't panic," she told herself. It was still broad daylight in a much traversed neighborhood. The youth would have to be desperate to try something foolish.

Desperate? Or just plain inebriated.

She torridly ran to her umbrella stand in search of her baseball bat, the same one Edna had pulverized Derek and Rashad with. The wooden bat had suffered a fracture during that melee but Jenna had wrapped it carefully with silver duct tape. She was shaking so badly, she dropped it at first.

Get a grip woman! Just think this through.

In between her howling sobs, Vicky had mentioned some cockamamie story about Kyle needing the money to plead for his life. Jenna rolled that off as just another attempt to coerce the frail girl into doing his bidding.

Vicky, sweet Vicky, when will you stand on your own?

She wasn't really surprised that Vicky had made contact with Kyle. Martin had warned her that it would be a tough pattern to break. Kyle was a reliable crutch, and with John Robinson gone, it would make sense for the girl to grip onto a familiar face. Jenna made a vow to herself to continue helping Vicky, not just with her addiction, but also breaking off her relationship with Kyle. The youth was like a slow moving cancer sucking the life from the teen's vulnerable psyche.

The apartment buzzer went off. Jenna jumped. Chuck snarled and barked.

"Damn," she whispered. She had fixed the lock on her door, but the speaker was still out of commission.

He's taunting me!

The building had been constructed centuries ago to house wealthy landowners. A peephole was unnecessary, and her modern day landlord had not seen fit to install one.

Jenna couldn't hear any footsteps on the stairway. Why would he skulk if he were going to enter his apartment? No, she was convinced Kyle was intent on searching her place for the cash.

She heard the sound of a key being inserted in the lock and saw the handle turn. Chuck made no move to assist her. Some help he would be.

She gripped the bat with all her might as the door opened slowly, and she saw a shadow cast across her floor.

A gun!

She felt like screaming, but her throat seized up on her. She felt like she might swallow her own tongue.

The person must have heard her gasping for air as the door swung open wider. Jenna felt her hands shaking. She stood to the left of the doorway, out of any peripheral vision.

I'm going down swinging! She told herself.

As the intruder entered, she closed her eyes and swung wildly at his head. The impact was tremendous. She felt her body vibrate on contact and heard the man fall to the ground in a crumple.

Thank god!

She opened her eyes to survey her conquest.

This time, the scream did escape her lungs.

Lying at her feet was the limp form of Sergeant Martin Conrad, a pool of blood emanating from the back of his skull.

"Marty!" she screamed. Jenna dropped the bat, and fell to her knees, cradling the wounded officer.

"What have I done?"

She couldn't lament her deed for very long. A second shadow came through the doorway. Jenna turned, lifting her bloody hands up to her face. Before her stood a black man dressed in a tan corduroy outfit. He had a gun in his hand.

Jenna tried to scream, but the man was too fast. He clamped a hand over her mouth and shoved her to the floor, her face inches away from Martin Conrad's unconscious form.

"Shut your pretty little mouth or I'll shut it for you," he ordered, kicking the door shut with his long leg. "He focused his eyes on the body of the police officer. "That's one big mutha," he muttered as casually as possible.

Chuck was barking as loudly as his breed could, but it was more of an annoyance than a threat. The man lashed out a foot, striking the Jack Russell, who whimpered and scurried off to the kitchen.

"You crackers always have those stupid dogs that ain't worth a damn," he noted.

Jenna said nothing. Her eyes were glued on the burly sergeant. Why don't you wake up and save me?

But Martin Conrad didn't respond, the pool of blood still seeping from his wound.

'"Please sir. Take what you want and leave!" she whispered.

Afro placed the tip of his boot on the back of her neck, grinding slowly. "I won't tell you again blondie! "

She closed her eyes, willing him to disappear.

"Open your eyes woman!" He dropped to his knees and placed the gun up against her temple. "Little jerk from across the way tells me you have my money. You hand it over now, and this ends. It's that simple."

"Take what you want and leave."

Jenna nodded. "Anything you want. It's in the kitchen cabinet. Inside a DSW shoebox."

Afro cackled. "Not very original." He looked down at Martin Conrad. "How the hell did the police have a key to your apartment?" he stood erect. "Unless, maybe you know this guy?"

"Please, he needs an ambulance. Take the box and go," she begged.

"Bossy little bitch aren't you?"

Suddenly, Martin Conrad had his arms around the man's legs. He yanked violently, sending the culprit head first to the wooden floors, but Martin was too weak to retain his hold. Afro kicked out violently, landing a blow to the big Irishman's face. Jenna could see his eyes cross before he sank back into unconsciousness.

"Damn you pig!" Afro barked with contempt. He drew his revolver and fired once. "You should have kept your big ugly head down. Now see what you made me do?"

The shot tore into the slumped form. Martin Conrad's body lifted momentarily, as if he had been jolted with electricity, before lying back down, unmoving.

"You killed him!" Jenna exclaimed.

Afro turned and leveled the gun at her. "You can mourn this boy or join him. You got three seconds to decide!"

Jenna didn't move. She stared at the lifeless form of her lover. Her jaw fell slack, tears welling in her eyes.

"One…" began Afro.

The girl remained motionless, numb to his words.

"Two…" his voice rained even louder.

Jenna didn't care. Not about him, not about anything. Not anymore. She only cared about the crumpled body of Martin Conrad. She was responsible for this. It was her blow that had knocked him out.

"He came to save me," she said, zombie like.

Afro would have none of this. "Get the money."

Jenna remained on the ground quivering.

"Bitch, you really want to die." He wound up and kicked her in the leg.

The pain barely registered with her. She struggled to her feet. "Kitchen," she muttered. "Shoebox."

"That's right. Cheap ass DSW shoes. Now get it."

Jenna strode to the cabinets in a trance. She opened the doors and removed the cardboard box. "Here it is," she whispered.

"Don't just stand there. Give it to me!" he demanded.

"Here you go."

Jenna hurled the box violently at her assaulter, the bills loosening from their rubber bands and scattering upon impact with his chest.

"You dirty.." He tossed his gun on the sofa and pulled out his blade. "I'm gonna do you with a personal touch."

Before he could open the blade, Jenna pounced on the man. Her eyes ablaze with anger, she ripped her fingernails into his face. Afro screamed wildly and dropped the blade. Blood streaked down his cheeks, blinding him. Jenna seized the moment and kicked him in the groin. He fell to his knees in agony.

Without hesitation, the girl located her bat and swung once. Her blow staggered the man, but he held sway, his arms groping out for her. Jenna couldn't avoid his hold. They tumbled to the floor in a heap.

"You little bitch…" Afro sunk his teeth into Jenna's forearm causing her to scream in agony, but she continued to struggle. She couldn't shake free from his grasp. He held her in front of him, their eyes locking. She could see the blood dripping from his wounds, and the manic glow in his eyes.

I'm going to die!

She head butted him viciously, just enough to break his grip. She was able to get to her feet and attempt to run but was thwarted by slipping in a pool of blood. Her body fell hard, the spill softened by Martin Conrad's motionless frame. He still had the apartment key in his hand. Jenna seized it, and rolled off his body.

Afro was still trying to recover from her head butt. She knew time was running out. Gripping the key as hard as she could, she swung her arm in an upward arc, and then rocketed it down toward his neck. The impact was so forceful, she felt her bones snap. Afro spasmed twice, the key protruding from his neck. It had embedded deep enough to puncture an artery. His eyes lost the manic glare, replaced by confusion as he choked on his own blood.

Jenna collapsed on her sofa and dialed 9-1-1.

Before her fingers could press a digit, Jenna felt her head snap back roughly. Someone had yanked her hair. Remarkably, her glasses had remained on during the brutal attack from Afro. She spun wildly to confront this new threat.

"Enough girl."

The voice escaped the lips of a stranger. He was a short, dark man of African descent. He wore a purple knit polo shirt. She had never seen him before.

"You have a lot of courage." He spotted her arm. It was twisted grotesquely. "That looks very painful." Purple shirt still clung to her hair. "Get in here boy!"

Jenna twisted her neck to see who he was talking to. Kyle entered the doorway, his face ashen with fear. She noticed the blotchy spot in his jeans. He had soiled himself. "You little creep!"

Purple Shirt waved a gun at the boy. "Hurry it up. Pick up that cash right now." He tightened his grip on Jenna. "Now we have to clean up this situation."

Jenna didn't answer. She gritted her teeth. One arm dangled uselessly, the other dripped blood from Afro's bite. Her immediate concern was to stay conscious.

Kyle remained frozen in his spot. "That's a cop!" He exclaimed, spotting Martin Conrad's body on the floor. "Holy Christ, man! This is Boston. Do you know what they do to cop killers? They'll rain holy hell on you."

Purple shirt snorted. "Not me. His killer lays in front of you. He has been avenged. End of story. Unless you wish to make it a trio, gather up those bills so I can leave."

"Don't be stupid Kyle. This man's not going to let us walk out of here," Jenna pleaded. "He might not shoot you now, but you know that's how it will end."

"I…" Kyle blubbered.

Purple shirt tugged on Jenna's hair, prompting her to stand on wobbled legs. "This boy can't help you. Look at him. He is weak, a mouse."

Jenna's eyes burned at Kyle. "Vicky didn't think so, Kyle. She trusted you."

Purple shirt released his hold. "What is this? Daytime soap opera? What is wrong with you white people?" He waved his weapon back in forth in a comically exaggerated movement. "This is a gun people." He pointed it at the two prone bodies on the floor. "Those are dead men in front of you. Do you not see the severity of your situation?"

Kyle turned to Jenna. "I didn't want this. I thought it would be cool to sell weed, make a few extra dollars," he confessed to her. "I screwed up."

"Enough boy!" Purple shirt fired his weapon. There was a loud recoil, and then Kyle dropped. "You were giving me a migraine."

A look of confusion surfaced on Kyle's face, as blood puddled from his stomach. "You shot me?"

"Yes, stupid boy. I shot you. Now lay there and die while I pick up my money."

Jenna couldn't believe it. Two shots had been fired inside her apartment. Yet no police, no sirens, no cowboy on a white horse. Nothing to dispel the idea that this wasn't real. Just the throbbing pain in both her arms. She crawled over to Kyle. "Let me see!"

She mustered up some energy to lift his blood soaked shirt. "Keep pressure on it. Help will be here soon."

Purple shirt laughed maniacally as he gathered up the money. "Ain't no one coming lady. See, way I figure it the police are no different than anyone else. They'll wait until the danger disappears and then they'll show. It's human nature."

Jenna stared at Martin Conrad's body. Not this policeman. He had rushed in without any regard for his own well being, surely blinded by his love for her.

She wobbled to her feet. "Give me a chance," she demanded.

Purple Shirt finished gathering the loot. "I beg your pardon?"

"Give me a chance," she repeated.

He smiled, intrigued. "A chance for what my dear? Should I hand you a gun and we can have a duel?" He laughed and turned his back on her. "This aint some damn renaissance fair."

Jenna knew her arms were useless. She rushed at him, hoping to catch him off-guard with a head-butt. It had worked on Afro.

He easily sidestepped her and she plunged past him, unable to stop her momentum. She tumbled madly into the kitchen.

Purple shirt was amused. "Damn feisty!"

Jenna lay helpless, flopping around like a fish out of water on her stomach.

"I hate you!" she moaned.

"I'm growing fond of you!" Purple shirt replied. "In fact, I'm starting to get a chubby." He grabbed a hold of her sweatpants by the waistband and yanked down, exposing her panties. "I think we have time for a deposit." He straddled her waist sitting backwards, his hand playfully slapping at her buttocks. "Not bad. You white girls gotta learn to eat. Fatten yourself up."

God, no! Please!

She tried in vain to prop herself up, but her arms betrayed her. This only served to further Purple Shirt's mirth. He ripped away her t-shirt and began working on her bra hook-latch. Jenna writhed in agony, unable to escape his clutch.

"Damn woman. I'm trying to make this comfortable for you." He yanked on her hair so violently, roots tore from her scalp. "Or maybe you like it rough?"

Jenna was face down, her cheek on the cold kitchen linoleum. She couldn't see her aggressor, but she felt his hands roaming up and down her back. It repulsed her. She prayed for a miracle. Edna with a bat or a machete. Some crazy thing like that. Or Grant Maxwell slamming a nice potted plant over her attacker's head, but when she felt her bra unclasp, she knew no one was coming.

"Please!" She begged.

"Be patient." He responded. "It will all be over soon." He tugged at the bra, violently tearing it away from her body.

Jenna flailed her legs blindly. She felt the back of her ankle strike bone. Purple Shirt grunted in pain. This gave her hope. She kicked harder and faster.

"Stop it bitch!" He clasped his hands together and chopped at her back like an axe. The force of the blow caused all the air to escape Jenna's lungs. Her body recoiled from the savage attack, as she gasped for oxygen.

In that moment, she was able to contort her body, flipping on to her back, and allowing precious air to seep into her lungs. Purple Shirt eyed her appreciatively. His gaze focused on her exposed chest. "You're gonna make me work for this, huh?"

Jenna didn't reply. She drove the elbow from her bitten arm into his ear. Purple Shirt howled in pain. The blow knocked him back on the seat of his pants.

Jenna pounced. Her legs free, she thrust her left foot violently into his face. Blood spurted from the man's lips, his head snapping back. He wiggled backward trying to recover, but she rained kicks on him. One caught him square on the jaw, chipping some teeth and sending shards into the back of his throat. He clutched at his neck, choking on his own blood and dental work.

Jenna brought herself up into a crouching position, kneeling in front of the wounded man's face. She lifted a knee to his jaw, sending him hurtling into the cabinets. She let out a primal scream. Purple shirt tried to shield his damaged face with his hands, but they merely slowed down the blows, as she pummeled him with feet and fists until he lay still on her floor.

Covered in blood, one arm dangling limply, Jenna picked up the phone again. This time she was able to complete the call. When the 9-1-1 dispatcher came on the line, she simply gave her address and quietly spoke "Send help."

She threw the cell phone with as much force as her tired arm allowed and crawled over to the body of Martin Conrad. She draped her body, still naked from the waist up, onto his chest and began to sob.

"Why Marty? Why you?"

She laid her head on his chest and closed her eyes, too drained to stay awake. She could hear a siren in the distance and footsteps on the stairway before she blacked out.

Jenna awakened to the now familiar bright lights of a hospital. She had one arm hooked to an IV; the other was encased in a cast. She groped blindly for her glasses.

"Looking for these?" The voice was obvious, the appearance wasn't. It was Marta Ruiz, sporting a bold new hairstyle. Gone were the long curly locks favored by her mom. Instead, she had a snappy shag cut. The glasses had also been replaced. She now wore contact lens.

"Marta!"

"Jennie!" She mimicked. "I'd hug you but the doctor said you're pretty fragile right now." She helped place the glasses on Jenna's face. "You're all over the news."

With her eyesight restored, Jenna took in her surroundings. She was in a single bed, private room. Over on the counter were several vases filled with flowers.

Marta nodded. "Mr. Maxwell sent the small one. The rest are from Mr. Esposito. I'd forgotten you named me and ma as your emergency contact. He called last night when he saw you on Channel 7.

"He said to tell you he and his wife are praying for you and to take as much time as you need to heal."

Jenna nodded absently, the memories of last night coming back into her thoughts. "It was horrible, Marta."

"Tell me about it. Thank god Martin showed up to save you. The police said he must have put up a battle to protect you. "

"Martin…he tried…"

"Tried, shmide. He saved you again."

Saved me? Is that what they think happened?

Jenna didn't really care. Truth was, Sergeant Conrad did try to save her. She bungled his effort, and he paid the ultimate price. And so had Kyle. "Marta, they're all dead. "

Marta resisted hugging her friend. "I know baby. They were bad guys. They deserve what happened to them."

"Bad? Kyle was a jerk, but not my Marty. He died because of me." She sobbed wildly.

Marta jumped up. "Died? No, sweetie. Martin's not dead. He's in the ICU. In fact, Mami is down there now with him."

"What?" Jenna was flabbergasted. *Not dead? How was that possible?*

"He is one tough man, I'll tell you that. Mami said they had to restrain him when he woke up. All he kept doing was yelling and trying to get out of bed to see you." She covered her mouth with a hand. "You poor thing. You thought he was dead?"

Jenna nodded, her whimpers starting to recede. "I want to see him."

"You will, Jennie. But not yet." She attempted to cheer her girlfriend up. "Well, what do you think of my new do?" She spun around like a ballerina.

"Beautiful," Jenna croaked. She was still absorbing the news regarding Marty. *Alive? Thank god.* "What about Kyle? Did he make it?"

Marta frowned. "Sadly, that scumbag is still with us. He's over at New England Medical or something." She paused, hands on hips. "Mami made me call your friend Vicky and let her know."

Jenna was taken aback. She knew how Edna felt about the troubled girl. It shocked her that Edna would respond so kindly. She was a never ending source of amazement.

Marta poured her a glass of water. "Drink this. I'll go get the nurse. And I had better go find Ma before she hooks up with one of those cute guys from BPD."

Jenna giggled. "Thanks. You really do look great, and slimmer if I may say so."

Marta sighed. "Mami bought me one of those body girdles from that store in Eastie. I can't breathe, but it holds my belly in."

"Stop, you're going to make me pee myself."

"Jennie?"

"Yes?"

Marta hesitated. "I called your parents." She waited. "Don't kill me. I just figured it would be better to hear it from me rather than some neighbor or something."

Jenna understood. "Don't sweat it." She drew a long gulp from her straw.

"God that's good. See if you can round up some food too. I'm starving."

"As you wish Miss Metabolism." She waved and departed.

Jenna felt the pressure on her bladder.

Screw the nurse! I need to go now!

She gingerly let her feet touch the cold sterile floor. Grasping the pole holding her IV, Jenna pulled herself up off the bed. She started to balance her weight on her numb feet when a shrill scream echoed behind her.

"Baby girl!" It was Edna Ruiz, splendidly decked out in neon green spandex pants that looked like they had been painted on, and a tight yellow halter top, tied at the mid-section. "You're awake." She scurried over to the bed, steadying Jenna in her arms. "Where in the hell do you think you're going?"

Jenna was overwhelmed with joy. "Edna, it's so good to see you." Even with the cast, she managed to wrap an arm around her friend. "How is he?"

Edna flashed a sardonic grin. "Now who would you be referring to? That handsome dog Chuckie? Or his manly master Martin?"

Jenna blushed. "I can't believe he's alive. There was so much blood, and the gun, and…"

Edna cut her off. "That man fought to the death for you. I heard his Captain say he might get a medal."

"Is that so?" asked a voice from the doorway.

It was Martin Conrad, modestly dressed in a hospital Johnny and a bathrobe two sizes too small. There were circles under his eyes, but other than that he looked no worse for wear.

Jenna stumbled over toward him, her circulation still not at a comfortable level. The big man caught her in his arms. She could hear him grunt in pain, but his smile betrayed any sign of it.

"I thought you were…" She began.

"Dead?" he guffawed. "No, I'm a Conrad. Remember? We get hit by cars or struck by lightning. No heroic ending for my type."

"You're really ok?" She asked, examining him with her eyes.

He balled a fist and raised it to his chin, imitating the famous thinker statue. "Let's see, I'm standing here breathing and holding onto the most beautiful woman in the world. Hmm. Yeah, I'd say I'm ok." He kissed her on the lips. "Doc says the bullet did some nerve damage, so I'll have some time off to heal. I made arrangements for Chuck. It seems he fell in love with those crazy girls when they took him home last night. I think they wooed him with Spanish lullabies. Anyway, Edna and Marta agreed to dog sit him for a while. "

"That's wonderful," she said.

"Jenna, I have to ask you this. Both of those guys were found dead. The Captain already told the press that I did it in self-defense while saving a citizen." He pulled her closer. "What really happened?"

She ran a hand across his cheek. "That blow must have given you amnesia. Don't you remember? After you got shot, you struggled with both of those guys. It all happened so fast and then it was over. And here we are." She kissed him. "That's all that matters."

Martin Conrad shook his head in appreciation. "You're a special lady, Jenna Coyne. What do you have to say for yourself?"

"I'm starving. Think I can borrow your gun? I need to rob a pizza delivery boy."

He wagged a finger at her. "I'd have to arrest you."

She laughed. "I don't think the handcuffs would fit over this cast. " She smiled intensely. "Can you do me a favor?"

"Name it princess."

"My parents are heading here, can you get them a parking spot?"

The burly officer tossed back his head. "Gotta love you Jenna. Gotta love you."

THE END

Cruel Winter

It was a harsh February night in New England, the kind where Mother Nature expressed her dominance over mankind. Jenna Coyne swung the door shut with as much force as she could muster. "God almighty, Marty, I've been ringing the doorbell forever!" She returned to the hallway to retrieve her grocery bags. "Didn't you hear me?" She stepped through the entranceway of the Charlestown apartment they shared and promptly fell on her face.

Startled, Martin Conrad woke from his slumber. "What happened?" He wiped the crust from his eyelids to reveal his girlfriend sprawled out on the kitchen floor, a casualty of his sloppiness.

"Not again!" the beautiful blonde shrieked, scrambling to recover her shopping. "You promised!"

She had tripped over a case of beer cans her boyfriend had left blocking the doorway. "They're warm! You didn't even refrigerate them!"

Marty shrugged and yawned. He was in his flannel boxers and a wife beater that barely stretched over his swollen beer belly. "Commence with the nagging. This is the part where you tell me I'm a lazy Irishman with a drinking problem."

Jenna gritted her teeth in anger. "Get off the sympathy kick. It's been eight months since you got shot. All you do is eat, drink and sleep. I'm tired of it."

Martin Conrad was a Sergeant for the Boston Police Department. He had been shot in the line of duty trying to save his girlfriend, Jenna Coyne. It was supposed to result in a storybook ending, and it had actually looked promising. The pair had fell in love and moved in together. All seemed right with the world.

And then it fell apart.

The rehabilitation was not going as planned. Martin's left arm never regained feeling, and he had been forced to accept disability compensation. For a second generation cop this was a death sentence. He had sunken into despair, ordering beer deliveries and watching old VHS tapes.

Jenna picked herself off the floor and went over to the television stand. She glanced at the screen. He was watching another black and white cowboy movie. They all looked the same to her. She turned the VCR off.

"Be careful!" Martin shouted. "That thing's sensitive." He stumbled over and hit the power button again and pressed eject. Unfortunately the tape jammed. "Fuck me sideways!" He roared. "That was my Pops' tape, you bitch!"

Jenna was in no mood for his crap. "You probably ruined it yourself, you drunken fool. Your Pops would be ashamed if he saw you now."

Martin's complexion grew even brighter. "You bitch! You're as cold as a witch's tit!"

Jenna was taken aback. He had never been this cruel and insensitive. "Listen to yourself, Martin! This isn't you. We need to call the doctor and get you some help."

He laughed and looked at her with a sneer. "I don't need a shrink. You're choking me, Jenna." He grabbed one of the beer cans that had rolled his way and popped it open. The froth and foam spewed everywhere. He guzzled the contents down, most of it splashing on his chest. He belched, crushed the can in his hands, and hurled it across the room.

"Marty!" Jenna's rage took over and she pounded on his chest with her hands.

The burly giant guffawed. "If you wouldn't mind, I'd prefer it if you hit me in the arm. That way I wouldn't feel it."

Jenna's anger evaporated. She felt a sense of defeat. This had been going on for the last three weeks, and the drinking had gotten worse. She couldn't deal with it anymore. She stormed into the bedroom and began to pack.

Martin staggered after her, thought better of it, and stopped for another can. "What's this? You going somewhere?"

She ignored him, focusing on packing her wheeled traveling bag.

"Talk to me Jenna." He grabbed her arm tightly.

"Let go!" she hissed. Before she had met Martin Conrad, she was a timid wallflower, but all that had changed over the summer when she had been abducted and forced to fight for her life. Jenna the mouse had turned into Jenna the lion. Self-defense classes had made her even more dangerous. She gripped his wrist, twisted down and to the side, hard enough to stun him but not break bones.

Martin yelped and dropped his beer. It landed on the comforter and puddled out. Neither one of them made an effort to retrieve it. "Fine, then," he said. "Pack your bags, take my car, I don't give a shit." He stormed out of the room in search of a fresh beer.

Jenna continued to load her clothing, shoveling it into the bag with reckless abandon. "Marty, you're drunk. Please let me call someone."

"Who you gonna call? Ghostbusters!" He retorted, laughing at the top of his lungs. "Where are you going? Your landlord let you break the lease in the North End. You've got no place to go." He chugged the rest of the contents of the can. "You can't go visit Edna and Marta because they went off to Brazil for three weeks."

Jenna ignored his inquiries. She regretted not asking her two best friends if she could tag along with them on their trip, but she hadn't wanted to leave Martin alone. Somewhere in the back of her mind she had seen this moment coming. Martin Conrad was too stubborn and too Irish to cope with the hand he had been dealt.

"Marty?" She had finished packing. She realized she had never even removed her coat. "I'm sorry it came to this." She waited for a response. None came. Martin kept his back to her. "I'm going to say goodbye to Chuck." She whistled. "Here Chucky."

A muffled yip emanated from the bathroom.

"You locked him up! You creep!"

Conrad shrugged, seemingly amused. "He wanted to watch his soap operas and he wouldn't stop that barking."

Jenna rushed to the bathroom and freed the Jack Russell terrier. The small dog raced over to his dish. "You lazy sack of shit! You starved him!"

Martin flapped his fingers wildly. "Nag, nag, nag. Fuck off already." He tossed her the car keys. His aim was off and the keys skidded along the kitchen floor. "You'll need those. It's too cold to fly your broomstick."

Jenna glared at him. "Give me a call when you straighten out your act. I'm going over to Vicky and Kyle's house."

"Wonderful idea. Shack up with a junkie and a drug dealer. "

"Well at least they acknowledge their problem, not like you. You've changed Marty. You're not the man I fell in love with. I feel like I don't know you anymore."

Martin Conrad stared at her. For a moment, she thought he was sober. "Get in line lady. I feel the same way about my stinking life. Do you think I really don't know what happened back there on Prince Street?" He was referring to the shooting. "It took a while, but the lab boys reconstructed the events. I didn't save you Jenna. I dropped like a sack of bricks when that bullet ripped through me. You killed those bastards. You were the hero." He started to sob. "You deserve that fucking medal the commissioner gave me."

Jenna tip toed over to him and grabbed his hands. "I thought I got what I deserved you big lug. Don't you see? You were all I wanted. I never would have stopped that attack on my own. You gave me the courage to fight back." She kissed him gently on the lips. "I'll never forget that."

"Jenna!"

She placed her index finger on his lips. "Don't say anything else. Sleep it off. I have to go, but remember this, I do love you." She grabbed her bag and departed.

"I love you too," Martin Conrad whispered.

The drive to Salem, Massachusetts only took a half hour, but it seemed like an eternity to Jenna Coyne. She had fought back tears, determined not to burden Vicky Sue Robinson with her problems. Lord knew, the young woman had a basketful of her own. A recovering heroin addict, Vicky was still struggling with the unexpected suicide of her father. She had immediately invited her on again off again boyfriend Kyle to share household responsibilities. Kyle had worked for her father's towing company, Black Cat Towing, and had lived in the same building as Jenna.

And, oh yeah, he was responsible for the entire mess that had led to Jenna killing two men in self-defense. That was eight months ago. It seemed like a different lifetime.

Vicky greeted Jenna warmly. The petite girl had come a long way since Jenna and Marty had sent her off to rehab. "C'mon in Jenna!" She threw her arms around the stunning blonde and hugged her affectionately.

Jenna noted the faint smell of cigarettes wafting off Vicky's wardrobe, but no signs of possible drug relapse. "You look fantastic, Vicky. " She didn't offer this appraisal haphazardly. The girl had been a grungy mess only months before. Now she stood before Jenna, looking fit and dressed sharply in clean clothing. Even her hair, which had been dull and thinning, had a playful buoyancy to it.

The same couldn't be said for Kyle. He still bore the facial scars that local drug dealers had inflicted on him that summer. He sat at the kitchen table, cutting up barcodes with a rusty pair of scissors. "Girl." Was all he muttered to acknowledge Jenna's presence.

Undeterred, Jenna offered a pleasant hello. The young red head simply grunted and returned to his task.

"Just ignore him." Vicky explained. "He's still up to his old tricks working schemes. You'd think he'd learn."

At this jab, Kyle's attention was peaked. "I'm doing this for both of us."

Jenna stared in confusion. "What exactly are you doing?"

Before he could answer, Vicky piped in. "The goof cuts out the label on low priced items and tapes them to expensive stuff, and then he goes through the self-serve line at the drug store. So far they haven't caught him."

Jenna covered her ears in exaggeration. "Stop already! Remember, I'm dating a cop." Her smile faded. "Or at least I was."

Vicky frowned. "I have to admit I expected this. The last time we came over, Sarge was really pounding them back. This stay at home stuff is killing him. Idle hands and all."

Jenna decided to change the subject. "So why the barcode scam? You guys hurting for cash?"

Vicky took the rolling case from her friend and moved it into the bedroom. When she came back, she threw up her arms. "The economy is tough. Kyle gets a good amount of tow jobs, but almost all the repo jobs Daddy use to collar are going to other companies."

Kyle interjected. "Plus, I'm not as good at it as Big John was. He scared the piss out of people. That's why he always got the repo jobs; they knew he'd bring back the goods."

"There's also the problem with the insurance company," Vicky noted. "Because daddy committed suicide, he voided his life insurance policy. We were hoping to use that money to make some repairs. As it is now, we can barely pay taxes and utilities."

"I still say he didn't kill himself," her boyfriend noted. Kyle got up from the table and got himself a can of soda. He didn't offer either woman one. He sat back down and returned to his task.

Jenna thought for a moment. "Maybe I can mention it to Mister Esposito, my boss at the insurance agency. Right now he employs a tow truck company as part of his package deals. Maybe you guys can get in on that business?"

Vicky beamed. "You are so amazing. You didn't come over here to listen to our sob stories. Sit down and take your coat off. It's time you let me return the favor for turning my life around." She glared at Kyle. "Finish that soda and run down into the basement and fetch one of those bottles from Daddy's stash he didn't think I knew about."

Kyle sighed and reluctantly got out of the chair. "Yes, because you're so busy."

Vicky didn't respond. She simply pointed to the basement door.

"All right!" the lanky red head pouted. "Be back in a few."

Jenna couldn't help but smile when Kyle sauntered off. She ran over and hugged Vicky. "I am so proud of you. The old Vicky would never have talked that way to him."

Vicky returned the smile. "The old Vicky didn't have any good role models like I do." She took Jenna's coat from her. "But don't change the subject. Sarge is a winner, honey. It might seem like desperate times right now, but don't give up on him. He's in a rut. I've been there."

"I know Vicky, but he's a loud, proud Irishman. He can't face the truth. That bullet destroyed the nerve muscles in his arm. He'll never pass a physical again. The doctors are positive."

"Big deal. Tell it to reader's digest." Vicky retorted. "Don't baby him, Jenna. Don't let him feel sorry for himself. I did that for all those years after I lost my mom, and trust me, it does nothing but turn your soul black." She went into the kitchen and rinsed two glasses. "You helped me. You can do the same for him."

Jenna hugged her. "Thanks, sweetie. I promise you I'll work on it."

"You'd better!" Vicky scorned. "I told you before Sarge is a catch. He's dreamy. You want to trade? "

Kyle surfaced from the basement. "Trade what?" he ventured.

Vicky laughed. "Were your ears ringing?"

"I only see two glasses." The youth responded, ignoring her question. "Aren't you going to have some?" He offered a dusty bottle of gin he had unearthed.

Vicky nodded. "Of course I am, but you're not. It's still early enough to get a tow job, and I want your skinny butt back in one piece."

Kyle pouted. In that instant, he looked ten years younger, and Jenna could sense the attraction between the pair. She was thrilled for the couple. They had been through the ringer, and their relationship had grown stronger. Perhaps Vicky was correct and things would work out with the disgruntled officer.

Vicky twisted open the bottle of gin. She stared at Kyle with a look of mischief. "You go upstairs and play video games while we ladies chat." Kyle nodded obediently. "And Kyle? Don't let those hands get too tired," she spanked him playfully. "Go on."

"And you…" she said to Jenna. "Go throw on your pajamas. I'll microwave some popcorn to go along with this rotgut Kyle found."

"Aye, aye," Jenna responded with a salute.

Jenna spent a wistful evening catching up with Vicky on current affairs. Vicky had remained clean and sober since coming out of rehab,

thankful that her addiction hadn't resulted in HIV or hepatitis. Kyle, too, had steered his way onto the straight and narrow, forsaking drug dealing and exhausting all his energy into maintaining the tow truck company. Unfortunately, the police had confiscated the forty thousand dollars he had uncovered during a tow, but Vicky had reminded him the consequences that had taken place because of his dishonesty. Jenna had almost been raped and murdered, and Martin Conrad had suffered a career ending injury. This had been enough to scare the two youths into going straight.

They had also made some cosmetic changes to the old homestead on Elm Street. Vicky had donated her mom's car to charity and cleaned out all remnants from the garage. No longer would it serve as a shrine to her deceased mother. They hadn't decided how to use it yet, but repairing the exterior was first on Kyle's list of home improvements.

The conversation about Vicky's mother had given Jenna pause to reflect on her own mother. She hadn't seen her since the incident. Jenna honestly couldn't recall much of their reunion. She was under heavy medication and still in shock from the attack she had endured in her small Prince Street apartment. She just knew it had been a long drive from New Hampshire for her elderly parents and she had barely spent any time with them before they had departed. All she could remember was her mother begging her to leave Boston and return to the safety of her parent's home.

Vicky had made a statement offhandedly. There was no tone of judgement, nor encouragement. She had simply uttered a phrase. "I wish I could see my parents again."

Jenna hadn't given it too much thought, the gin and popcorn distracting her contemplation, but the next morning and all through work at Esposito Insurance Agency, the words kept drifting in and out of her conscience.

I wish I could see my parents again.

She had mentioned the idea to her employer about taking a couple of days off to see her parents. She wasn't sure he would go for the idea. She had missed a lot of work after her hospital stay, not to mention the multiple absences related to assisting Sergeant Conrad in his rehabilitation. Despite this, William Esposito agreed to time off without hesitation.

He still feels guilty.

In a moment of weakness, eight months ago, he had sexually harassed Jenna in the workplace. She probably should have reported it, but at the time of the incident, she was still the timid newbie fresh out of college and desperate for work. She had forgiven him, and much to her relief, nothing like that had ever occurred again. But obviously, William Esposito hadn't forgotten his transgression, as he always agreed to her demands. She almost felt guilty about it. Almost.

Now driving home on the snow covered streets of Charlestown, she had only to convince Marty to make the trip with her.

When she opened the door this time, Jenna was cautious to look down and make sure nothing blocked the entrance. Much to her relief, the case of beer had been removed.

Or finished?

She heard the faint echo of the television, the volume low, but loud enough to distinguish that a Spanish channel was playing. That was a good sign. It meant Chuck was watching television, and if he was watching television, that meant he wasn't locked up again.

Chuck only viewed Spanish language programs. This had been the case ever since Martin Conrad rescued him from certain euthanasia at the city's animal shelter.

"Marty, you ok?" she called out tepidly.

Chuck heard her but didn't even turn his head, mesmerized by whatever program he was viewing.

"Marty?" she tried again.

Sudden panic set in. Oh my god! Did he fall and hit his head?

Jenna raced into the bathroom, her heart pounding. She tugged back the shower curtain. It was empty. She hadn't realized she had been holding her breath. She gulped in a large amount of air.

"Thank god," she whispered aloud.

"Thank him for what?" A voice responded from the kitchen doorway.

She pivoted just in time to see Martin Conrad enter. "A policeman's girl should know better than to keep the door open like this." He admonished. He had a bag of Chinese takeout in his arms. All signs pointed to sobriety.

Chuck cocked an ear toward the conversation but still kept his eyes on the television set, his body firmly planted on its familiar resting place, the coffee table.

Martin wiped his feet on the doormat and entered the tiny kitchen area. Jenna remained glued in place outside the bathroom door. Neither spoke. They looked like two gunslingers ready to hash it out. Finally, the rugged officer broke the silence.

"I thought I'd give you a break from cooking tonight." He waved a hand

...the case of beer had been removed.

at the takeout bag. "Not the healthiest choice, but tasty as all damn."

Jenna relaxed her pose. "How'd you know I'd be back for dinner?"

A coy smirk surfaced on his mouth. "Because I'm irresistible?"

Her face remained rigid, emotionless.

Martin Conrad placed the bag on the table and walked over to Jenna. They had played this scenario out before. Unfortunately, it was becoming as stale as a sitcom re-run. He would apologize and Jenna would forgive.

"Jenna, last night..."

She raised a hand to him. "Stop, Marty. I'm not mad at you. I'm just confused. I've tried understanding your problem, but I can't get a grip on it. There are so many people worse off than you. For God's sake, you were there, at the Marathon. You saw what happened to those people! "

The officer shrugged his bulky shoulders. "I remember." He hugged Jenna, as he had a thousand times. "I know I have a problem. I can't put it in words."

She hugged him back. "Try."

He let out a whoosh of air. "When Pops got hit by the car, I made it into a challenge so I could cope with it. I pretended like I was some knight on a quest and I would become a policeman and take care of my family." He yanked off one of his boots. "It's all I ever thought about. Mom said I was obsessed. I guess she was right. Look at those scratchy video tapes. I've practically worn them out. The stories they tell are so simple, literally black and white. The good guys have to defeat the bad guys. To me that was the summary of life. I didn't give a shit about sports or music or anything growing up. I just wanted to be that good guy that defeats the villain, except I didn't."

"Go on," she prodded.

"The villain defeated me. And you were the good guy. If you weren't there that animal would have emptied the rest of his clip into me, and to be honest sometimes I wish he had."

Jenna stared at him in disbelief. "Why Martin? Don't you realize how selfish you sound?" She crossed her arms and pursed her lips. "I get it now. This macho crap. It really tears you up that a woman saved your ass. Well let me tell you something, buster, get off your pedestal. Because, believe me I would have preferred it if you had swooped in and rescued me. Did you ever think about my feelings? I killed two men. People told me weeks later they could still see blood on the cobblestones!"

Marty's face contorted in a myriad form of expressions, confusion, guilt, anger and finally understanding. "It's not easy for me to say these words, but baby I'm sorry."

"You should be."

"I'm sorry I forgot to get duck sauce."

After a moment, Jenna wound up like an old time pitcher and punched him in the right arm. "I'd hit the other arm, but I don't feel like watching you cry, you big jerk!"

Marty smiled at her gleefully. "I could arrest you for assaulting an officer."

She grinned back. "The charges would never stick."

"Is that so?"

She nodded playfully. "I'd be forced to tell them about your handcuffs and your night stick and how you forgot to read me my Miranda rights."

"Miranda? Another one of your sexy Latin playmates? Invite her over. I still have one good arm."

Jenna punched him on the left side. "Bring it on copper!"

He curled her into his arms. "Chinese always taste good reheated. What do you say we go fool around?"

"Mister Conrad, what are you implying?"

He placed his hands on her slender hips. "I think it's time you work off this month's rent."

She giggled and kissed his nose. "Only if you grant me one wish"

He wagged a finger at her. "Now I have to add bribery to the charges against you." He unbuttoned the top of her blouse. "Let me guess. You want me to go back to physical therapy and try to revive this dead hunk of flesh?"

"Yeah." She answered, undoing the next button. "But that's not what I was going to ask. I think we need to get a way for a couple of days."

Marty arched an eyebrow. "My great powers of deduction tell me you already have something planned."

She finished unbuttoning her top. She let it fall open, revealing her bra. "Tomorrow morning we leave for New Hampshire. I think it's time my parents meet you."

The burly giant stared at her tight abdomen. "How did your body get like that and mine looks like this?" he asked pinching his flab.

Jenna helped him pull his shirt over his head, careful not to show too much attention to his damaged arm. "Maybe city life is making you into a soft pretty boy?" she teased.

"Pretty? Maybe. Soft?" He pulled her toward him. "I don't think so."

Jenna grabbed his hand and pulled him toward the bedroom. "C'mon,

Sergeant. You better enjoy this because my parents are old fashioned. You'll be sleeping on a sofa the next couple of days."

Marty laughed and tickled her, prodding her toward the bed. "You have the right to remain silent..."

After dropping off the dog with Martin's sister, Jenna insisted on stopping by Grant Maxwell's flower shop the next morning, even though it was out of their way. The air was frigid and the sidewalks hadn't been cleared, but Martin Conrad knew better than to argue against the idea. Instead, he remained composed, the car idling as he double parked and patiently waited for his girlfriend to run into the Post Office Square establishment.

From his vantage point, it was clear Jenna and the old man shared a mutual friendship. He glimpsed them embracing before the wizened proprietor unveiled a huge flower basket filled with brightly colored blooms that had no business surviving in the brutal New England frost. Marty smiled as he saw the old timer wave off Jena's advancement of money. Instead, she gave him another hug and then retreated back to the car with her oversized gift basket.

"Should I be jealous of Mr. Maxwell?" He kidded.

Jenna shivered, happy to rejoin the warmth of the car. "He's a sweetheart. Truly my best friend downtown and always full of good advice." She giggled. "Plus, he's cheaper than a therapist."

Marty shifted into drive and carefully made his way into traffic. The brutal weather had frightened most of the traffic away, and they made the leisurely trip out of downtown without incident.

"It must be nice," he said. "I mean, having so many good friends. Grant, Edna and Marta, even Vicky and brain dead Kyle. You've got a cult following, lady."

Jenna nodded in understanding. "That's a handful compared to the crowd you hang with."

"The force? Those are brothers and all good people, but not friends in the true sense," he reasoned. "I guess you're my only real friend."

"I don't know about that. The mailman got a hernia carrying your get well cards." Jenna replied. "But I get your drift. I am lucky to have met those folks. Once you see Franklin you'll know why I don't have too many hometown buddies."

The Franklin she referred to was Franklin, New Hampshire, home of her parents. Only a couple of hours drive from Boston, it was a small fishbowl of a town that still bore resemblance to 1950s Americana. She felt a smile surface just thinking about it. Jenna wondered why she had waited so long to return.

"Penny for your thoughts?" the big man queried.

"Just thinking about my mom and dad. They were so good to me. Mom always said I was her little miracle." She saw his look of interest and continued. "Mom was in her mid-forties when she gave birth to me. And Daddy, well, let's just say he has quite a few years on her, so it must have been a shock when I finally popped out all those years later.

"They were so possessive, it was almost strangling me. I mean, they never let me out of their sight at all. No gymnastics or girl scouts or any of that and certainly no sleepovers. It's almost like they were jealous if anyone else spent a moment with me."

Martin shrugged, never taking his eyes off the road. "Just making up for lost time. I see it with cops all the time. Guys are never home much and when they do get to spend time with their kids, they end up smothering the poor little bastards. Your folks probably felt something similar."

Jenna simply nodded. She closed her eyes in comfort. It was nice to converse with Martin. The tension of the last few weeks appeared to lighten with each mile they drove, and she could sense a change in her companion. Martin's stress seemed to disappear whenever he was occupied and the treacherous driving actually seemed to relax him. He hadn't mentioned his arm the entire drive, and he had driven past several liquor stores without even glancing at them.

The traffic was light and Jenna prompted him to stop at the outlet mall a few exits from her home. She loaded up on cans of coffee for her Dad and Martin had suggested pastry. She vehemently forbid it. Jenna's mom was a proud cook and there would be no store bought bakery items in her home. Instead, they settled on a carriage full of crescent rolls and other desert items they could conjure up later.

Twenty minutes after departing the strip mall, they arrived at the tiny town of Franklin. If you blinked, you would miss the main street. It contained a few, restaurants, a couple of gas stations, a laundry mat and several retail sites, not all of them open for business.

"Where do they hold the square dancing?" Marty joked. "Look at this place honey. I'm expecting to see Andy and Barney show up in a squad car."

Jenna remained upbeat. "I thought all you men secretly dreamed of meeting the farm girl in the hayloft? "

He grinned. "Just please tell me I don't have to cook over an open fire?"

"Of course not!" she retorted. "Daddy would never trust a city boy with his barbeque tools." She gripped his hand tightly. "I can see my house!"

The house in question did nothing to allay Martin Conrad's preconception. It was a huge rectangular homestead that appeared to be an old horse barn that had been converted to living quarters. "Jesus Christ." He mumbled. "Did your grandpa's grandpa build this?"

Jenna snorted. "Isn't it wonderful? It has that prairie house look, but believe it or not, it's all modern. It's a prefab that Daddy had centered on this land right before I was born. It's just designed to look like Abe Lincoln built it."

Marty whistled in exaggeration. "Good. Because I thought for a minute I was gonna have to hunt dinner and I didn't bring my rifle, just my service revolver."

A look of anger came over Jenna. "Seriously? You took your gun? Please leave it locked in the trunk, Marty. I don't want to give my parents anything to worry about."

Martin was about to defend his decision when the door to the home swung open. A frail looking man exited. He wore a thick brown sweater and heavy wool pants. Wisps of white hair covered most of his bald head and he walked with a hunch. He stood motionless at the door for a moment until recognition set in.

"My baby!" the old man trotted to the car, his hands waving by his side. Jenna rushed out to greet him, nervous that he might take a spill on the slippery ground.

"Hi daddy!" she beamed at him, hugging him while steadying his awkward pose. "Daddy, you shouldn't have come outside. It's freezing and where's your coat?"

The old man squinted and waved his arms at Marty who was still seated at the wheel. "Well. C'mon, don't make me catch pneumonia!"

Martin stifled a grin. He liked this feisty geezer already.

"Daddy be nice," Jenna warned. "Martin's a cop remember?"

Martin exited the vehicle and stood erect in front of the old timer, his hand outstretched. "Nice to meet your, sir."

"Big son of a bitch, ain't you? No wonder you crushed those bastards tried to hurt my little girl." He slapped Marty's hand out of the way. "Can't shake your hand. Hell, can't even shake my dick dry. Arthritis and all."

Marty nodded. "I can relate."

The old man paused and then glanced at the burly giant. "Right, you took a load of buckshot in the arm." He slapped at the arm playfully. "Must of been like a mosquito bite to someone of your size. Now c'mon get in the house. You can get your bags later. I want Mom to see you before she takes her afternoon nap."

Jenna shrugged at Martin who winked back.

Welcome to the family!

The interior of the Coyne home was modest. A worn sofa occupied the center of the living room. Opposite it, stood a large picture tube television. The rest of the room was decorated sparsely. Thomas Coyne ushered them into his abode.

"Daddy, it's roasting in here!" Jenna exclaimed, peeling off her parka.

The old man shrugged. "Tell me about it. Mama doesn't like the cold these days."

"Where is she?"

Arching a thumb toward the staircase, the elderly man answered. "Upstairs sleeping. She's had a rough time lately."

Martin Conrad's police training kicked in. He could tell something was wrong. "Is there anything we can do?" he offered.

A frown spread over Jenna's face. "Daddy, what's going on? Mom knew we were on our way up here to visit."

Thomas Coyne arched his hips back and placed his hands behind his back. "Sit down kids. We need to talk." He waited until they sat on the sofa before continuing. "Honey, I didn't want to talk about it on the phone, but your mother's been having medical issues lately, and…"

"Issues?" Jenna interrupted. "Daddy, what are you keeping from me?"

"I'm not keeping anything from you. I'm telling you now if you'll let me continue." He scolded. "She hasn't been feeling well lately and I finally persuaded her to see a doctor, and…" he threw up his arms. "I'm no good at this crap. Listen, Jenna, they found cancer in your mother."

Jenna sat motionless. Finally, Martin spoke up. "Is it treatable, sir?"

"Doctor said there is a chance if we can find a bone marrow match."

Jenna blurted out. "Why didn't you call me sooner? You know hereditary matches are the most successful?"

Thomas Coyne averted his eyes. Again, Martin Conrad's police instincts kicked in. "I think your dad is trying to explain something to you, Jenna."

"You should listen to Sherlock, honey."

Jenna felt her head spinning. "Daddy, you're not making any sense. What the hell is going on?" Her face was turning red with anger and frustration.

Marty grabbed her hand. "Let him finish."

Jenna's father came closer to the sofa. She could see tears had welled up in his eyes. "Baby, you're not going to be a match for Mama."

"What? Why?"

Martin Conrad knew the answer before it escaped the old man's mouth. Every vibe in his body told him that Thomas Coyne had been harboring a deep secret. Finally, he spoke up. "It's ok, Mr. Coyne. Jenna needs to hear it from you."

"Hear what? " her voice was a shriek. She felt like cursing at these two men in her life who kept exchanging covert glances at one another like they were members of a secret society.

"Jenna," the old man whispered. "I'm not good at this crap. I'm just gonna preface this by saying your mother and I love you."

"But?" she pried.

"You're not our daughter!"

The rest of the evening passed by in a blur for Jenna. She vaguely recalled listening to her father spew a weak story of the Coyne's vain attempts at fertility having failed so often that adoption had become the only alternative for the couple. She had sat through the speech, never making eye contact with her father.

There was no anger, only confusion. Why the big secret? There was no shame in adoption. The entire spiel had left her with a nagging suspicion that her father was harboring even more secrets regarding her origin.

The old man had simply finished his explanation and departed for bed. No apology. No hint of guilt or anger or any emotion. It was if he had been describing an old program he had watched.

Jenna sat in a well-worn recliner opposite the sofa which was serving as Martin Conrad's sleeping quarters. The burly cop was on his back, hands behind his head staring at the high ceilings of his girlfriend's childhood home.

"Well, say something!" Jenna prodded.

Marty sighed. "You may not like it," he grunted. "Listen, Jenna, I know this came as a surprise to you, but it's not the end of the world. You're adopted. Big deal. Right now that man has bigger issues. His wife is dying and you still haven't gone up those stairs to see her."

Jenna frowned. "Don't make me out to be the villain. I didn't forget about Mom. I'm honestly afraid to see her." She got up and joined him on the sofa. "This is too much for me right now. You've dealt with this before. I've never lost anyone."

"Who said anything about losing her? People are beating cancer every day. "

She clutched at his hand. "I know, but this is my mom we're talking about."

"Jenna, go upstairs and see her." He said in a commanding voice.

Jenna nodded. "I will, I promise, but it is late." She raced across the room and reached under the coffee table to grab one of the photo albums. She flipped through the pages until she came across a photo of her parents from a few years back. She handed it over to Martin. "This was taken freshman year of high school. Mom and Dad drove me every day."

Marty smiled at the photo, happy that it soothed Jenna's attitude. "Got any with you in it? I want to see pictures of you in your farm girl overalls."

"Okay dirty old man," she joked. "But it wasn't like that. I was daddy's princess. He wouldn't let me lift a finger or get a drop of dirt on my dress." She headed back to the coffee table and withdrew one of the older albums. "I've been spoiled since birth."

Jenna sifted through the plastic pages until she located the photo she was seeking. "Here it is."

"Here what is?"

She pointed at a photo of her parents standing in front of their car holding infant Jenna. Scribbled underneath the photo was a caption that read: Jenna's first day home.

"That was me when they took me home from the hospital, but I guess we know now that isn't what happened."

Martin said nothing. He simply stared at the photo for what seemed an eternity. Jenna began to get anxious. She had seen that look before. It was the look a police officer assumes when confronted with a statement that didn't seem factual.

"It's definitely not right after your birth." He saw her puzzled gaze. "The baby in this photo is at least a year old."

Jenna didn't question his statement. His trained eye was usually accurate on matters of description. "But that is the first day they took me home. I always just figured they meant from the hospital. I never guessed I had been adopted."

Marty continued to stare at the photo with an intensity that frightened Jenna. "There's something bizarre going on here." He pointed at the trees in the background. "No leaves. And look closer, you can see snow on the ground."

Jenna shrugged. "And why do you feel the need to mention this?"

Martin sat up. "Maybe it's nothing, but ask yourself this. Why are your parents outside on a snowy day without coats on?"

"They left them in the house?"

"Possible but not likely. Especially if they were bringing you home from somewhere. Plus why is the car parked so far from the entrance? If you had a new baby wouldn't you pull up as close to the door as possible?"

Jenna shrugged. "Go on. I got nothing."

"My gut reaction is that it's not their car. Someone else drove you here."

"Like who? You mean my real parents?" Jenna started to feel dizzy. "Come to think of it, that's the only photo of that car I have ever seen. My dad drove a Buick Century," She squinted harder at the photo. "So who does this car belong to?"

Martin rubbed his chin. He hadn't felt this invigorated in months. "My guess would be the one person missing in this photo."

Jenna waited. Finally, she gave up. She slapped hard at his knee. "You mean…?"

"Yes, the photographer."

They heard a deliberate cough on the staircase. It was Thomas Coyne. He wore a robe over his pajamas. He eased his way down the final steps. "I guess my baby was right about you city cops. Clever man you are."

"Daddy," Jenna whispered. "I just want the truth. The only thing that matters is that Mom gets better."

Coyne nodded and cleared his throat. He went into the kitchen and grabbed three shot glasses and a bottle of scotch. "This is going to take some time, and I have a feeling you kids will need this."

He proceeded to tell Jenna the missing details of her origins. Martin's suspicions had been correct. The photo was taken many months after Jenna's birth, and the car did belong to the photographer, but it wasn't her natural mother. The Coynes had never met the young woman, nor did they know her name.

"Well that's normal with adoption." Jenna stated matter-of-factly. She was shocked by her father's terse reply.

"I never said you were adopted!"

Turned out that adoption was an avenue that the Coynes had turned their noses at. They shamefully feared being placed with a minority child and both parents were adamantly opposed to that path. They had opted for a different acquisition. They had purchased her.

"A surrogate?" Martin Conrad inquired.

Again, the elderly man shocked them with his reply.

"No, I said we bought you."

He refused to go into details, citing that it no longer made a difference. She was a Coyne. They had loved her and raised her as if it had never mattered.

Jenna continued to badger her father. Was it consensual? Did the mother want to give up her baby? Was there a father involved?

Thomas Coyne never wavered. His answer remained the same.

"What does it matter? You're my daughter!"

"Only, I'm not!" Jenna thought. When she continued to press her father for answers, he grew angry and then tired. Eventually, he left them to ponder this bombshell of information.

Jenna was torn between a flurry of emotions. Anger, humiliation, confusion. It was a cycle of overwhelming feelings blanketing her frail psyche. She bolted out of Martin's arms, past her arthritic father, and into the bed of her sleeping mother where she lay sobbing next to the sickened woman until finally exhaustion took over and she passed out curled up to the woman who had raised her.

Jenna awoke the next morning to an empty bed. Her mother no longer lay next to her. The sheets were cool, indicating the woman had left some time ago. Bolting from her prone position, Jenna took the stairs two at a time.

The living room was void of life. The only hint of occupation being the roaring fire churning in the fireplace. A solitary coffee cup stood guard on an end table. Jenna lifted it and felt the outside. Cool to her touch. It must have been consumed much earlier. Her eyes narrowed, remembering where her parents kept the clock. There was a small hanging Swiss clock above the mantle. It informed her that it was well after eight am. Afternoon time for New Hampshire folks.

Disgusted by herself for sleeping so late, she sped off to the kitchen expecting to see her parents finishing up breakfast with her boyfriend. It too was bare. Not a sign of anyone. She peered into the sink. Empty. No coffee mugs nor dishes.

What's happening?

She stood motionless straining her ears to detect any presence. All she could hear was the soft scraping of a shovel outside at the neck of the driveway.

Must be daddy!

She tugged on her parka, not bothering to zip up and slid her boots over her worn socks before unbolting the side door and heading out into the frosty air.

Her first step landed in a few inches of snow. Mother Nature had dropped her load on Franklin overnight. A smooth blanket of white fluff blinded her as she scanned her surroundings.

"About time you got up." Martin called out, his face red from exertion. He was struggling with a shovel full of snow in his right hand, the left barely gripping the handle. "You've been living the easy city life for too long woman. The mountain folks are already halfway through their day."

Jenna was in no mood for games. "Where are my parents?"

"If you talking about the Coynes, they left over an hour ago." The gigantic sergeant responded. "They didn't want to wake you."

"Where did they go?" Jenna asked, her voice tinged with confusion and worry.

Martin stopped shoveling and came over toward her. She could the ice clinging to his eyebrows. He kissed her gently. His nose was frigid and gave Jenna a case of the shivers.

"Are they okay, Martin?"

He nodded. "Yes, your mother didn't sleep well so they took a ride over to Tilton. Is it far?"

"Not really, just the next town over." Jenna finally zipped up her coat. "Martin, did she say anything? About last night?"

He smacked his lips together. "Nope. In fact, your father decided not to even mention it. After you went to bed last night, we talked for a while and he feels it's best not get your mother involved. He'd rather she go to her grave not knowing that you found out about it."

Jenna pondered it over and shrugged. "I guess I owe her that much, but I'm not going to let it rest, Martin. My real mother may be out there somewhere, and I have a right to know."

"Agreed," was all he offered.

Jenna took stock of her man. He was a tall Irishman, proud and fearsome in appearance. He had recently put on quite a bit of weight from his beer binging, but not so much as to be all flab. He still maintained the handsome profile of a rugged cop.

"Not use to digging out your own spot?" she teased. "Big tough guy has the condo association plow your tiny parking spot for you."

He grinned. "Tell me about it. I've been out here for over an hour. Your old man came out, warmed up his truck and drove right off."

Jenna decided to press her luck. "I suppose you're going to blame your bad arm for this taking so long?"

"Not at all," he spit back. "In fact, I've been resting it in case you got your sorry butt out of bed."

She arched an eyebrow. "Resting it for what?"

"Well, I'm not sure what you apple farmers call it up here, but we Townies like to refer to it as a snowball fight."

Jenna whistled sharply. "You wouldn't dare!"

Before he could respond, Jenna struck first blood, burying her boot deep into a pile of snow and lofting it into the big man's face.

Stunned, Martin Conrad bellowed loudly, wiping the cold from his eyes. "Oh that's how it's going to be." He charged her and tackled her, careful to shield her body from harm.

"No fair!" she cried affably. "You're supposed to throw the snow, not the person."

He pinned her to the ground and pressed his lips upon her. "Do they have hot showers here?"

She made a tortured face. "What if they come home?"

"Tell them it's physical therapy. Tell them it's a city thing."

The rest of the day was uneventful. Jenna's parents returned, reluctant to discuss their early morning trip and adamant that they would prepare the Sunday dinner. After a brief argument, a compromise was struck. Jenna did most of the preparation, guided by her mother's watchful eyes. The elderly woman appeared hearty and vigorous, only her pale skin and decaying hair betraying her health. She neither complained nor commented on her condition, instead choosing to focus her energy

Jenna did most of the preparation...

on cooking and maintaining a casual, but honest conversation with her daughter.

After everyone's belly was filled with a delicious oven cooked meal, and in the men's case, quite a bit of alcohol, everyone settled back in front of the fireplace to watch some old movies. Martin was ecstatic that Thomas Coyne maintained a huge inventory of video cassettes, many of them paralleling the big man's obsession with old westerns. They had already finished the bottle of scotch and had moved on to something else.

Jenna idled her time pouring through the photo albums with her mother, eager to bring up the subject of her birth, but each time squashing her desire for information. Instead, she forced herself to be content with the knowledge that her parents had raised her with love and admiration. Occasionally, the subject of cancer reared its ugly head into the conversation, but her mother downplayed the graveness of the situation, relegating it to her husband's overactive imagination.

The talk soothed Jenna's fragile nerves, and before long she was able to let go of her nagging suspicions and just enjoy the company of her parents. She even got them to agree to allow her to keep a few photos from the albums. Jenna only coveted the one shot featuring the car that had dropped her off at the Coyne home. But to be less conspicuous, she grabbed a good dozen or so.

When she could see her mother's energy level waning, Jenna aided the elderly women to her bedroom and helped her into her night clothes. She couldn't help but let a gasp escape her lips, when she cast her eyes on her mother's gaunt body. The clothes had hidden the condition well, but now free from their restraint, her body couldn't cloak the disease that was eating away at it. Jenna choked back tears, and put on a false front, as she dressed her mom and helped her into the bed.

The sound of the television blasting from downstairs told her that the two men would be fine in each other's company, so Jenna slipped underneath the covers with her mom.

"Goodnight, Mom," she whispered.

William Esposito licked his lips wildly with anticipation. Despite the treacherous drive, he had looked forward to going to his insurance agency this brisk and chilly Monday. Jenna would be returning from her sojourn to New Hampshire. Young, sexy Jenna, the object of his infatuation, the thought of her flowing blonde hair filled him with tingly warmth.

He had arrived an hour earlier than usual. It allowed him to beat the traffic and escape the early morning nagging of his ever depressing wife. She was a decent enough soul, putting up with his shenanigans and over active libido. That was the other reason he had ventured out so early. He wanted to relieve himself before Jenna arrived.

He entered his cozy office and locked the door. He tore off his ear muffs. He wouldn't wear a hat. It might mess his toupee. It was cold and the air tasted stale from the weekend. He quickly turned up the thermostat and then draped his coat over a chair instead of the hook he had installed on the back of the door and proceeded to his chair. He didn't bother turning on the lights nor opening the blinds. Stealth would be required for his morning ritual.

Without hesitation, he unbuckled his belt and dropped his trousers. Underneath, he wore a pair of shimmering pantyhose. His wife was aware of this perverted habit. It didn't seem to bother her. He was a good provider and a quiet, unassuming man. If he chose to indulge in fantasies, she was all for it as long as no harm came from it. In fact, she often surprised him by coming home from the mall with extra pairs.

After running his hands up and down his thighs and over his ass cheeks, he began to grind his palm against his genitals. He already had an erection. That was why he loved the pantyhose. It allowed him to maintain a constant state of arousal without revealing a vulgar bulge. He hadn't seen Jenna in a couple of days and he was over eager to explode. When he felt himself reaching climax, he removed his shaft and ejaculated on his desk. His load was tiny. His wife had given him a surprise hand job only an hour before. She said it was a reward for being patient with her mood swings. He didn't care what the reason was, as long as he could pop off under the caress of her soft fingers. Satisfied with his output, he wiped his tip with a tissue and pulled the pantyhose back up before drawing on his pants again.

Forty-five minutes later, Jenna entered through the main doorway, her face reddened from the cold. He could see her breath in the air and imagined what it might taste like if breathed into his mouth. Esposito greeted her with a freshly brewed cup of coffee and listened intently as she filled him in on her weekend activities. She was dressed warmly in a thick sweater and woolen slacks, but this didn't detract from her natural beauty. Esposito felt himself getting distracted from the conversation wondering how long before he could unload again.

He did pay enough attention to consider the idea of adding Black Cat Towing to his list of services. He already outsourced towing to another company, but had a feeling Kyle and Vicky could be persuaded to join him at a much lower rate. Times were tough, and he was already being taxed with the burden of Jenna's inflated salary. He had given her a bump in pay after feeling a sense of guilt from inappropriately touching her last summer. Jenna had forgiven him, but he didn't want to chance a lawsuit, and besides, he felt she was worth every penny just for the sheer physical joy of viewing her body on a daily basis.

When the conversation shifted to Jenna's early childhood, his interest perked. He craved to learn as much as he could about his gorgeous assistant. Was she always this beautiful? Were there other hot women in her clan? When Jenna displayed the photo of her arrival, he suggested scanning it in so she could enlarge the image.

"Great idea Mister Esposito. Maybe I can make out the license plate?"

He nodded enthusiastically, his eyes glued to her buttocks as she leaned over to insert the photo. He felt his loins begin to stir, and averted his eyes briefly in shame.

After a couple of tries, the image was sent via email to her desktop computer and Jenna was able to enhance the photograph clearly enough to make out the license plate number. She was thrilled when Esposito offered to research it for her. He had access to the national database and could retrieve data going back decades. Within ten minutes, he had obtained a name and address.

Jenna was ecstatic. "You don't know how much this means to me!" She hugged him fiercely, and he could feel the swell of her breast beneath the sweater. "I can't wait to get back up to New Hampshire to check this out."

"Why don't you go tomorrow? " Esposito suggested. He felt himself getting a chubby from their brief encounter. "I could arrange for your two friends to come in and discuss business, and I'm sure they could help out if it gets crazy here."

Jenna wanted to jump up and down. "Thank you sir. Thank you so much."

No, thank you, William Esposito thought.

William Esposito memorized the happy expression on his assistant's face. He planned to recall it later at lunchtime when he would occupy the office by himself.

«—»

The insurance records indicated the car was registered to a Lilith Hannigan, of Manchester, New Hampshire, from 1988 to 1994. A phone call from Martin to BPD Headquarters produced very little information. All he could manage was to confirm the address that Jenna's boss had supplied.

"Do you know anything about this Lilith?" Jenna pleaded.

Martin sighed. "The address no longer matches her residency. I checked it out and it belongs to an elderly section eight couple who have been living there for the last five years. I was able to track down the building owner, and he couldn't recall when this woman, Lilith, had lived there."

Jenna was frustrated. Her anxiety was causing her to shake. "Marty, this woman might be my mother! She couldn't have fallen off the face of the Earth. She has to be out there somewhere."

"I know Jenna, but she didn't leave a forwarding address, and it has been almost twenty-five years. She could have moved out of state or even passed on. My godfather promised to run her social through the databases, and see if he gets a match, but I have to be honest with you, it's a longshot."

"Thanks. Talk to you later." She hung up the phone, and then slapped her forehead. She hadn't bothered to thank him or even tell him she loved him.

Distracted, she poured herself another cup of coffee and turned on the computer. She would have tried to watch television, but she was in no mood to deal with Chuck and his obsessive viewing habits.

Lilith Hannigan.

The name flowed through her thoughts as she tried to browse through her emails. Jenna sorted among the usual spam and friend requests for a few moments before giving up. Martin was downtown with his fellow officers, and Vicky and Kyle were too far away in Salem. A smile drifted across her face as she thought of Marta and Edna Ruiz bathing in the warm sun in Brazil. Marta was probably wearing a long t-shirt over her suit, while her mother would most assuredly be tanning topless under the gaze of lusty men.

Jenna chuckled to herself, and decided to call a cab. She would go visit Grant Maxwell, the florist. His calming voice always soothed her nerves.

The cab ride was better than a ride at an amusement park. The driver never slowed down, despite the icy roads, and treacherous snow drifts. This pleased Jenna as she was unable to focus on her own problems, survival being her main priority at the moment.

When the journey finally came to a halt, Jenna mumbled a sarcastic thanks and tossed a twenty to the driver. She didn't bother waiting for change. She hoped the extra dollars would give him pause to stop for a coffee and maybe put a few less lives at risk.

Grant Maxwell greeted her at the door. She had called from the cab, nervously wondering if he had decided to close up for the day, but his gruff voice on the phone assured her only a weak man would let such a pitiful snowfall hinder his day,

She wasn't sure how old he was. Each time he seemed to add a few more years to the total. She guessed he was in his early sixties, but the corded muscles in his neck and back of his hands, revealed he had been a brawny man in his youth.

He hugged her gently and ushered her into his shop. "Come in Gina!" He never called her Jenna. She had long ago stopped trying to correct him.

She shared her tale over a steaming cup of Earl Grey. She was shocked that he hadn't offered coffee. "My quack doctor thinks I should cut back on caffeine, so I started drinking this stuff." He lifted his tea cup, a souvenir from the North End. "I have to admit, it's not bad on a cold day, but I still have to make twenty trips a day to relieve my bladder."

Jenna sipped at her tea, relaxed among the presence of her old chum. She wished all her troubles away, and secretly found herself daydreaming that Grant Maxwell was her true father. Blushing, she wiped the image from her mind, and related the adventures of the last few days.

Mr. Maxwell listened intently, interrupting frequently to verify facts, and nodding each time in confirmation. "You know sweetie, we didn't have computers in my time. When you wanted to find someone, you did it the old fashioned way … on foot."

"What do you mean?"

He shrugged. "You're what twenty years old?"

"Twenty-three," she corrected.

"Excuse me, practically a senior," he spat back. "Anyway, that's not a longtime in the big picture. You've got an address and a name. Someone has to remember this Hannigan woman."

Jenna nodded. "I agree, but what do you suggest?"

"Well, I know it's colder than the Russian front, but get off your butt and hit the streets. Knock on doors, and see if someone remembers this woman. After all, she might be your mother."

"My boss did say I could take a few more days, and besides I think I just found a way to increase his business by setting him up with Black Cat Towing, so he owes me."

Grant Maxwell drained his tea. "Besides, that big guy of yours looks like he needs some exercise. " His face turned somber. "The arm still killing him?"

"Not literally, of course. Some people have had amputation because of gunshots, but the docs are confident that Martin can regain mobility in his arm, if only he would go to rehab."

"He will. It's in his bloodline, honey. Besides, even one armed, that boy could take on Paul Bunyan!"

Jenna giggled. "Thanks, Grant, you always cheer me up. I'm going to pursue this lead and see where it takes me."

"Be careful, Gina."

She hugged him. "Tea suits you."

He waved her off. "It's for British pansies. As soon as you leave I'll brew a pot of good old fashioned American Joe!"

Jenna spotted her cab across the way. Thankfully, it wasn't the same driver. "Go home, Mister Maxwell. No one is buying flowers today."

"It's all about having a routine, Gina."

Turned out Grant Maxwell may have been a bit of a prognosticator. Several of the residents in the Manchester neighborhood did, indeed, remember a Lilith Hannigan living in the area many years back. No one recalled a baby girl. In fact, no one recalled ever seeing her pregnant.

The information Jenna obtained was random, and not of much use. It appeared Lilith Hannigan had rented the apartment for a short number of years, where she had resided alone. No one remembered a husband or boyfriend at all. In fact, if not for the car she would have been a blip in their memories.

Lilith had loved that car, the same one in the picture that Thomas Coyne had handed over. It was a 1988 Lincoln Continental. She had purchased it shortly after renting the apartment. The neighbors had found it odd, because the girl showed no signs of income, and hardly ever ventured out. But when she did leave, she made sure everyone noticed her fancy new car.

"Oh yeah, she'd give anyone a ride to the supermarket or drugstore. Lilith loved showing off that car," one neighbor remembered.

Jenna had little success finding anything else concerning the mystery woman. Neighbors assured her she had not been pregnant during that time period, which would rule her out as a possible birth mother. Still, Jenna was intrigued, and her relentless desire for information forced her to push on.

It was only after a couple of slices of pizza at the corner shop, that she hit pay dirt. The cook behind the counter, his apron covered with sauce, recalled seeing Lilith several times in his shop. He was positive because her name was unique, at least to him, and she frequented the place often enough to have been recognized.

The cook was an older man and he seemed sincere. Jenna had no reason not to believe him when he said that Lilith Hannigan often came in to meet a man with children.

Jenna prodded him for more details.

"Well, I remember it clearly because it always stuck out as being odd to me."

"What did?" Jenna asked.

"The guy was always the same, young, rail thin, maybe a biker. Or at least he dressed like one. You know, chaps, and all. What made me take notice is he always had different kids with him. Some were infants, sometimes girls, sometimes boys, but never the same kid."

Jenna continued to prod. "What were they doing?"

"Nothing really, this guy would come in and she would hand him packages. Clothing, diapers, that kind of stuff. He didn't say much, and he was very quiet. I remember the girl asking lots of questions, but the guy would always hush her and then give me a death stare. Now, I'm an old man now, but back then I wasn't afraid of anyone. You have to be tough in this neighborhood, but I'll admit, I was afraid of that dude. I couldn't relax until after he left."

Jenna had absorbed the information carefully, questioning the man's appearance again, but the cook couldn't offer more of a description than he already had. He was almost ready to go back to his pizza preparation when he offered one more tidbit.

"He paid for that car. Must have been in the envelopes he always handed her. The girl never opened them, but she always dressed well, and that car didn't come free, so I assumed he was some sort of sugar daddy."

"She was a prostitute?" Jenna whispered, annoyed at her repulsion.

The cook wiped a line of sweat from his brow. "Maybe, I don't know. She seemed like a straight cookie, not a junkie or anything. I never seen the two of them as much as hold hands, never mind kiss or anything. You could just tell something was wrong. And I keep going back to those kids. Must have been at least a half dozen different ones. None of them over the age of five or so, if I had to guess."

Jenna thanked him for his time. Her head was spinning. What was the secret of Lilith Hannigan and her gentlemen friend? Was she a drug mule? Were they running a daycare? All kinds of thoughts ran through her mind.

She checked her watch. It was getting late, and the drive back to Boston would take longer under these weather conditions. She would do one last circle of the neighborhood and then head back to Charlestown and hope that Martin Conrad had dug up some information.

Martin Conrad was sitting at the kitchen table drinking from a can of beer when Jenna got home. She scowled at the open can, but offered no opinion. A quick scan of the trash, revealed no further empties. She followed up with a search of the fridge, relieved to find a six pack with only one ring empty.

"Go easy on that," she said.

"Hello to you too. " The big Irishman responded. "I've been worried sick. The forecaster called for another snow storm tonight, and I wasn't sure if you'd get stuck up there."

Jenna ignored his comment, and opened a can of dog food for Chuck. The Jack Russell bolted into the kitchen as soon as he heard the lid pop off. "How's my baby?"

Chuck greeted her with his usual burst of energy before tearing into the bowl.

"I ate already," Martin Conrad proclaimed.

"I was wondering if you were going to polish off the rest of that beer for supper." Jenna threw her parka onto the sofa and collapsed at the kitchen chair. She immediately dived into her recollection of the day's events.

Martin had listened intently, interrupting her once to replace his beer with a fresh one. He gave her a smug look before settling down on the sofa.

Jenna was just about to begin a rant about his drinking when he surprised her.

"I think I know who the mystery guy is."

Jenna felt her heartbeat stop, and it seemed like she had to will it to start back up.

Marty winked. He had caught her off guard.

"While you were out catching pneumonia trying to imitate some fifties gumshoe, I was at home beating a path the new way, with my fingers." He gestured at the laptop on the coffee table. "A little bit of research told me that this Litlith Hannigan had a brother, who fits the description you gave me. Real bad ass. Drove an expensive Harley, and of course, never worked a day in his life."

Jenna snatched the can from her boyfriend and guzzled the remainder. Much to his surprise, she fetched two more, cracked them open, and handed him one. "Go on, Sherlock."

Marty took a big gulp and let out an exaggerated burp. "Seems the brother is well known in both states as well as Rhode Island. Has a record in all three. Minor stuff, mostly misdemeanors, but he never served time."

"Tell me his name!" Jenna demanded.

"Easy girl, I was working my way up to it. David Hannigan, age forty-eight."

"You got this all from the police files?"

"Hell no!" Martin snorted. "Most of this stuff was out there on the internet. Just ran your friend through and came up with some hits. No address for her, but big brother Davey just bought himself a brand new bike, and sure enough he posted the dealer's name on his facebook page. My buddies at the station are making a few calls right now. I'll have his address before we go to bed."

"He has a Facebook page? Is my mother, I mean, Lilith on it?"

Marty nodded. "She is mentioned, but I don't think she is your mother. If she is, she has changed a lot."

"What do you mean?"

"Well, for one thing she's married. And her wife's name is Sharon."

Jenna ran for the laptop. "This should be good."

Say what one will about social media, but in this instance Jenna Coyne was happy to be part of the electronic age.

The images of David Hannigan oddly recalled the description the pizza chef had recalled from almost twenty five years ago. Sure, he had lost some hair, and crow's feet edged out from the side of both eyes, but the wiry man still possessed an image that projected menace.

Most of the snapshots displayed on the web featured Hannigan posing aboard his pride and joy, a metallic steel horse he had christened, El Diablo. Jenna shook her head in amusement. Her former college roommate, Marta, would have gotten a kick out of the irony. Here was this fearsome Irish biker who had dubbed his ride with a Spanish name.

Still pencil thin, David Hannigan came across as anything but frail. His arms were cabled muscle, the tendons snaking from the skin like the lines on an old pirate's map. His mustache was of course a handlebar. The entire package would scream stereotype if Jenna wasn't so frightened.

She flashed through the albums, hoping to catch a glance of his elusive sister Lilith. Much to her despair, she uncovered only a handful of scantily clad floozies.

She found it odd that there was no mention of children. Not one single photo of a child could be found among the various folders.

What about the children at the pizza shop?

Her concentration was interrupted by the buzzing of Martin Conrad's cell phone. His fingers glided over the screen before he lifted his eyes to meet hers.

"What is it?" she asked.

"I've got an address on the guy. Or at least it's what he listed when purchasing the Harley. Seems our guy still lives in Manchester."

Jenna glanced at the clock. It was an hour before midnight. Too late to depart for New Hampshire.

"I want to go there, Martin. I need to know if his sister is my mother."

Martin nodded. "Me too." He didn't mention that he was more interested in finding out why the pair had continually brought children to the pizza shop.

Mother Nature was still on the rag, dropping another couple of inches on Boston overnight. Martin toiled with a shovel, his damaged arm hampering the cleanup, while Jenna rounded up supplies.

They had decided to pack enough clothes and gear for a few days with the intention of heading back up to Franklin, regardless of any information they may have discovered.

Thomas Coyne had phoned an hour before. His wife had taken a turn for the worse. Seems cancer might not claim her at all. Congestive heart failure had decided to take a stab at the deed.

Jenna's emotions bubbled over. She wished she hadn't been so abrupt with the old man. Sure he was brash and over bearing, but he was a product of his generation. Too stubborn and racist to adopt a child of color, and too proud to admit he may have been sterile; the man had taken drastic measures to fulfill his wife's dream of motherhood.

Jenna shook her head, angry with herself for trying to romanticize the situation. Morals aside, what they had done was wrong. No young woman should have the right to sell their child, regardless of the situation.

She wondered if Lilith Hannigan had regret.

Does she even know me?

Did she cut out clippings from my childhood?

Did she know I graduated from Stonehill?

Does she know I killed two men?

Jenna felt her head spinning. She had to dispel such notions until she knew more. Maybe this wasn't her mother? What did she really know about her? There had been no photos on her brother's Facebook page, only a cryptic remark regarding his sister.

Under one photo, David Hannigan left the disgusting comment, "everyone was present except for my dyke sister and her wife Sharon."

Jenna would have missed the line completely, if not for her boyfriend's trained eyes.

Did it mean Lilith was gay? Or was it just a brutal display of Hannigan's ignorance? Did it even matter?

She found Chuck staring at her. It was clear he knew travel was imminent again.

"Sorry buster. I know we just picked you up from aunties, but momma has to go back out again."

The Jack Russell yipped twice in formal protest.

"Stop it, Chuckie. A couple of days without Telemundo won't kill you."

She peeked through the kitchen blinds. Her sight landed on Martin, still struggling to shovel snow away from his car. It was odd seeing someone so powerful look completely helpless at such a minor task.

A year ago she would have been terrified to interrogate someone like David Hannigan without the protection of a fully abled Martin Conrad, but now she didn't give it an after-thought.

Only days after the attack, Jenna had resigned herself to the fact that evil did exist. She had met it head on and survived through sheer will and a bit of luck. She had immediately decided to better her odds should such a situation ever arise again.

Along with the dynamic duo, mother-daughter team of Edna and

Marta Ruiz, she had enlisted in self-defense classes taught by one of Martin's former academy friends who had gone on to have some success in the mixed martial arts business. As a result, Jenna no longer felt helpless. In fact, staring at the man she loved, she felt supremely confident that she could protect herself and her man.

She rapped on the window.

Martin looked angry, but forced a smile when she stuck her tongue out at him.

"Pick up the pace, Sergeant. I'm not paying you detail wages!"

The burly Irishman heaved a scoopful of snow toward the window. "You're not paying me at all, lady."

"That's right, I forgot. You're on the dole now!"

Martin laughed out loud. "Want to switch places? I can make a sandwich just as fast as you can."

She tried to think of a snappy comeback but couldn't. She was just happy he had awoken in a good mood. The drinking had put a damper on their lovemaking the last few weeks. The tension had grown so bad Jenna contemplated ending the relationship. Fortunately, the trip to see her parents may have saved the couple.

Staring out at the struggling giant, Jenna couldn't imagine a life without him.

The snow had finally halted its descent from above. This did little to dissipate the hazardous travel conditions. Black ice and an overbearing reflection from the glare of the storm proved dangerous for Martin Conrad. Eventually, he gave in to Jenna's pleading to take over the driving, but not until after two close calls on the highway.

Not until after reaching their exit, did either occupant feel safe. Fortunately, the public works department of Manchester had no problem battling the snowfall. The streets were clean and manageable.

The proud officer cautioned Jenna about approaching the Hannigan's homestead. These people were unknowns, and already a caution flag had arisen from what few details they had obtained.

Jenna agreed to downplay her curiosity. Truthfully, she only sought the specifics of her origin. Whatever lifestyle or habits that David Hannigan possessed meant nothing to her. She was only interested in his sister, Lilith and whatever role she may have played a quarter of a century ago.

The address his peers had supplied caught Martin Conrad by surprise. He had expected an apartment building in the modest city, but a Google search had displayed a modern family home, not a hint of sinister foreboding.

They kept the car idling at the top of the street. The heat was cranked and both were dressed warmly, but Jenna still shivered uncontrollably.

She had no idea if David Hannigan knew his sister's whereabouts. His cryptic remark about her sexual preference led one to conclude there may have been some animosity among the siblings. Jenna couldn't let that stop her. She just wanted to make contact with the woman who may or may not be her natural mother.

Martin pointed to a vacant parking space three doors down from the Hannigan house. Jenna nodded and put on her blinker. She pulled into the spot which had been neatly shoveled.

Immediately, a door opened from the home adjacent to the sidewalk. A middle aged woman came out in her bathrobe and a pair of hastily pulled on boots. She had curlers in her hair and a cigarette dangling from the crook of her mouth.

The woman began waving frantically at them.

"Don't think you bastards are going to park there?" she shouted in a shrill tone, almost dropping the smoke from her lips. "My Eddie shoveled that spot for an hour."

Martin rolled down the passenger window. He was familiar with the unwritten laws of snow removal. A space was usually reserved with a chair or a bucket, and it was a longstanding tradition to honor the effort or risk having your tires slashed or windshield cracked.

"I totally understand," he said. "Is it okay if we use it for a couple of..."

He never finished the sentence.

The door from the house swung open again. This time a man emerged. He must have taken the time to gear up because he had the full winter outfit on.

Martin figured this must be Eddie.

"Look, we were just going to leave." Conrad shouted.

The man was covered in a flannel hunting jacket over a thermal shirt. His head was adorned with a wool football cap. In his hands he held a shovel menacingly.

"Damn right you were. God damn Massachusetts assholes think you run the world." The man spit out from tobacco stained teeth.

Martin held his temper. "I said we were moving."

Eddie's grin widened, revealing a set of uneven choppers. He hawked up a snortful of phlegm and spit on the windshield.

"Oh no doubt about that dipshit. You and your whore ain't parking that heap in the spot I cleared out. This ain't liberal Massachusetts where you fags are protected."

He held the shovel out horizontally like a hockey player waiting for the puck to drop.

Jenna could see the skin redden on her boyfriend. She knew that look could only mean trouble.

"Let's go Marty."

Eddie nodded. "Listen to your bitch, Marty. She may just have saved your fat hide."

He tapped the windshield lightly with the shovel.

Jenna began to put the gear in drive when Martin Conrad gripped her arm. "No."

Before she could protest, the proud Irishman swung open the car door with his right arm.

The middle aged woman who had remained silent during the exchange became animated.

"Fuck em up, Eddie!"

Eddie started to advance, but Martin was already out of the car. With his good arm he grabbed at the shovel and pulled it down and away from the attacker. Eddie didn't let go, and his momentum thrust him forward into the officer.

Martin lifted his knee and brought it up under the man's chin. The force of the impact was immediate. A sickening noise echoed down the street as teeth mashed against each other, and Eddie was sent sprawling to the pavement. Martin never removed his grip from the shovel.

The woman began shrieking and bellowing for help to emerge from the house. Within moments two teenagers came rushing down the path wielding aluminum baseball bats.

Martin remained calm, the shovel still in his hands as he raised it defensively, ready to ward off any attacks. The two youths weren't dressed for the weather. One was in his bare feet. They charged at Martin with the intention of attacking, but after staring at Eddie rolling in the snow, they halted their pursuit.

The seasoned officer had experienced this type of situation before. The boys would not attack. They were scared and only needed to save face. The situation was calming down.

He was wrong about that.

While Martin was focusing on the immediate threat in front of him, the woman had circled behind the burly man. During the melee she had armed herself with a ceramic lawn ornament which she intended to crush Martin's skull with.

She may have succeeded too, if not for Jenna's quick intervention.

Jenna had sprung from her seatbelt and exited the car during the initial encounter with Eddie. Now she calmly whacked the ornament out of the woman's hand and immediately twisted the arm behind the woman's back.

Jenna shoved the woman up against the door of the car roughly, but it was unnecessary, all the battle had gone out of the woman. She stood weakly, sucking in lungfuls of air.

"Let me go you twat!" she pleaded. "Look what you did to my Eddie!"

Eddie was sitting up now, his jacket drenched with blood. The two teenagers were doing everything in their behalf to stem the flow.

Martin feared the man had bitten off his own tongue. He rushed over to assist the man but was waved off.

"Don't touch him!" one of the boys pleaded. "Haven't you hurt him enough?"

Jenna released her grip on the woman.

"You need to call an ambulance for him."

Martin Conrad grabbed her shoulder with his numb left arm and pointed to the car. "Let's go. We can clear this up with the police later, but right now we are drawing way too much attention."

Jenna looked up. The sidewalks were filled with bystanders. A couple of houses down, she saw a long haired man staring from the doorway. It was David Hannigan. He had enjoyed the spectacle.

Manchester's finest showed up shortly later. Not offering up much protest, Martin Conrad was cuffed and hauled away. Much to her relief, Jenna was allowed to go free.

She drove away from the scene carefully, still shaken from the incident. Martin had spoken very clearly to her. He instructed her to contact his godfather, the precinct Captain, in Boston and explain what had happened.

Jenna did as she was told and listened carefully to the policeman's orders. When he had finished, he politely asked her to repeat back to him what he had requested. Much to her chagrin, Jenna could not parrot his

"Let me go you twat!"

advice back to him.

The Captain did not berate her. He simply repeated his comments until she was able to recite what he had told her. His casual tone helped soothe her nerves, and after a few minutes she was clear on what needed to be done.

Jenna was to head out away from Manchester and grab a bite to eat. Some time would have to pass before the men in blue could straighten out the problem. The Captain assured her that Martin would be fine. He even joked about the burly Irishman popping his cherry, but Jenna failed to grasp the humor of the situation.

She drove for twenty minutes until coming alongside a familiar chain restaurant. She parked, entered the establishment, and ordered coffee and pancakes.

Forty-five minutes and three refills later, the Captain rang her cell phone. She heaved a huge sigh when learning that Martin was ready to be released, and that all had been cleared up. Apparently, Eddie was a frequent visitor to the Manchester Police station and had an existing warrant out for his arrest. He had politely declined to press charges.

Jenna shoved her plate out of the way, the pancakes untouched and waved the waitress over to cash out.

Not too long after, she was sitting in a police station listening to a squad of men exchanging war stories with her boyfriend.

Martin had stripped off his sweatshirt to show off his bullet wound. The scar still frightened her.

She smiled politely at each officer who made a point to tell her how lucky she was that Martin Conrad had been there to ward off her attackers last summer.

If only they knew the horrid truth. It had been Jenna, herself, who had knocked the Sergeant out with her own baseball bat. This had led to Martin being shot, and Jenna left to defend herself against two savage men intent on killing her.

Somehow, someway, she had survived that day, in the end, covered with blood and surrounded by corpses.

Boston Police were unable to comprehend or more likely unable to acknowledge such a feat. Instead they had conveniently labeled Martin as the hero, showering him with medals and acclaim.

For several months, the big man was unaware of the farce, having believed his own hype that somehow he had defeated those monsters before falling victim to exhaustion and blood loss. The truth had only started to surface recently and had spiraled Martin into his depression and heavy drinking.

It was nice to see him, laughing with his peers, enjoying his time in the spotlight.

Jenna wished he had never found out the truth. It would have been better for all if the story remained uncovered. She didn't need the validation to know that what she had done was miraculous. It had happened, against her wishes, and she desired nothing more than to move on.

After the spotlight of a visiting hero started to diminish, Martin said his goodbyes and departed with his girlfriend. He still beamed with satisfaction from the fact that he could still handle himself, despite his newfound handicap.

Jenna teased him slightly.

"Did they fingerprint you and take a mug shot? Can I get a copy?"

He laughed wildly. "Crazy girl, my Godfather will never let me live this down. I'm in for it when we get back to Boston."

Jenna grabbed his arm as they made their way back to the confines of his frozen vehicle.

During the drive to Franklin, Martin filled her in on what he had uncovered during his brief incarceration.

It seems David Hannigan was well known to the best of Manchester's police department. The police had supplied him with valuable information regarding this criminal and his elusive sister.

Hannigan didn't work, had no visible means of income, yet he owned his property outright. No mortgage payments necessary. The property was bought and paid off, same thing for that shiny new motorcycle. He had simply paid it off with a cashier's check.

While Jenna found all this economic information intriguing, it was the man's criminal record that made her stomach somersault.

Five years ago, David Hannigan had been involved in an altercation in a local tavern which had resulted in the death of a young college student. Charges of manslaughter were filed against Hannigan. Apparently, he had struck one fatal blow to the drunken brawler, rupturing the carotid artery, and killing the youth. The trial had resulted in a verdict of not guilty; the defense able to convince the jurors that Hannigan had acted in self-defense.

Manchester PD warned Martin Conrad to beware of encountering the biker. All indications pointed out that he was a fearsome brawler and a skilled fighter. It would be noteworthy to avoid a physical altercation with the subject.

Jenna sat dejected as Martin relayed the information to her. Not once had he mentioned the sister, Lilith. After she prodded him for knowledge, he confessed, the New Hampshire police had little to offer regarding the mystery woman.

"No address, no phone number. She hasn't filed taxes in years. She hasn't renewed her license at the RMV, absolutely no trace of the woman," he informed her. "At least she doesn't have a criminal record."

Jenna took little comfort from this last speck of information. If this guy was her uncle, she'd be better off forgetting about any family reunion.

The thought of family shook her back to reality. She accelerated a bit, careful not to fishtail on the black ice. She needed to get home and see her real mother. She only prayed that Thomas Coyne had exaggerated the woman's condition.

Martin Conrad seemingly read her mind. "It will be okay, honey. Your dad won't let her go without a fight."

Thomas Coyne greeted them in the waiting lounge of the local hospital. Only days had passed since Martin had been introduced to the feisty old-timer, but he could plainly see a huge difference. The man looked ragged and worn, raccoon circles around his eyes. If anything, one would have assumed he was the one suffering from cancer.

Jenna was reassured that her mother's condition was not fatal. She had been rushed to the hospital as a precaution against pneumonia. The doctors originally had suspected heart failure, but tests proved inconclusive. Cancer had riddled the woman's immune system and even the slightest ailment could ravish her body.

Thomas Coyne spoke swiftly, his usual swagger depleted. He apologized for inflating the situation, but Jenna and Marty waved off his apology.

Jenna decided to confer with the doctors, herself. Their explanation didn't satisfy her nagging doubts. No, her mother hadn't suffered a heart attack, but her body was still deteriorating far too quickly. The doctors suspected the original cancer diagnosis may have been too optimistic. The disease was chewing up cells too rapidly.

The woman would be gone within days.

Never before had Jenna felt so secure in her childhood home. The earlier encounter with Hannigan's neighbors was still resonating with her. She sat on the sofa, legs curled under her, observing her boyfriend stoking the fire. Martin had insisted on doing the task, and surprisingly Thomas Coyne didn't protest. The old man had nodded glumly and padded off to the kitchen to fix himself a late snack.

The house had been frigid, the heat turned below normal. Martin feared the pipes may have burst, but a quick search proved that notion false. He was on his knees, still wearing his winter coat while he slowly fed the flames.

Jenna stared intently at the big man, noting how childish his profile appeared at the moment. He looked like a child at the zoo feeding one of the predatory animals from a distance, scared but too proud to admit it. Yet her mind refused to erase the image of Martin shattering Eddie's jaw. She had never seen that type of rage exude from him, not even during his worst drunken tirade.

The Irish cop must have felt her eyes on his back. He shifted and waved her over.

"I think you might be better off sitting close to the fireplace until this house warms up," Martin suggested. "It may take some time."

Jenna didn't answer. She simply rose and moved closer. Her eyes watched the flames dance. It was soothing and hypnotic.

"I don't care anymore."

Martin's brow furrowed. "About what?"

"Lilith Hannigan. I don't care anymore."

Martin didn't respond. His police intuition kicked in. He knew when to press a subject and when to sit back and let the information gather. He spun his back to the flames and sat quietly.

Jenna glanced toward the kitchen, assuring herself that her father was out of earshot.

"It doesn't matter if Lilith is my birth mother. I have a mother, a wonderful mother, and that man in there," she pointed at the kitchen. "He is my father."

Martin gave her a single nod, but he did reach out with his bad arm. In her mind, she could see the scar that the bullet wound had left. It angered her that he had suffered such an imperfection because of her mistake.

In the movies, the hero always shrugged off the bullet wound, wrapping a towel or a torn shirt over the hole. The credits would role and the matinee idol would return in the next feature as good as new, never to mention the incident again.

It hadn't turned out that way for Martin Conrad. His injury had baffled Boston's finest doctors, all of them echoing the same hopeful prognosis.

Give it time.

But they had given it time, plenty of time. Eventually, Martin had been forced on worker's compensation, his days of active service coming to an abrupt halt.

Jenna had never believed it true, until recently. Her eyes filled with tears recalling him struggling to push the snow from his shovel one handed. She shuddered thinking how fortunate he had been to defeat angry Eddie. She watched him now, tending to the fire, his body slumped to one side. She was overwhelmed with guilt.

"We need to go home, as soon as my mother is better."

"You're tired right now."

"Yes, I am, but my mind is made up. Forget about this wild adventure. No good can come of it."

"It already has."

Jenna looked bewildered. "What do you mean?"

Martin draped an arm over her shoulder. "It's brought us closer together." He kissed her softly.

Jenna responded eagerly, her lips locked with his.

The sound of a throat being cleared broke up their moment. It was Thomas Coyne, holding two tall glasses of whisky.

"Thought you kids might need to get your blood flowing, but I see you had other means of doing that."

Jenna laughed. "Thanks, Daddy. " She grabbed one of the beverages and handed it to Martin. "You keep the other one, Daddy. I'm going to fill up the bath tub and check in with my girlfriend, Vicky."

Thomas Coyne nodded and helped his daughter up. He let his grip linger. "I'm glad you came home, baby. "

She hugged him fiercely. "I am too."

Jenna had revived herself with a lukewarm bath and a mug of cocoa while confessing all her anxieties over the phone to Vicky. It was usually, ex-roommate, Marta who caught the brunt of Jenna's long winded conversations, but she was off vacationing with her mom, Edna. Much to her surprise, Jenna realized that Vicky was starting to fulfill that role.

Vicky had listened sympathetically, offering up her services in any way, while also informing Jenna that Mister Esposito had agreed on a contract with Black Cat Towing. Much to her happiness, Vicky would be commuting to the insurance agency on a daily business to schedule clients for Kyle. Bill Esposito had even suggested an older gentlemen who would work with Kyle on the repossessions.

They had chatted for almost an hour, reassuring each other that the future would promise good fortune for both young ladies.

Jenna hung up the phone, feeling more confident about her situation. Immediately, the phone rang again.

It was the hospital. They had been calling the line for almost a half hour. The Coynes did not have call waiting, feeling it was an unnecessary feature that catered to the impatient. Thomas Coyne would regret his old fashioned ways.

The young doctor who had telephoned did little to disguise the concern in his tone. He made it abundantly clear that Mrs. Coyne's condition had worsened, and it was time for the family to say their goodbyes.

Jenna was floored. She had changed into pajamas after bathing, thinking it would be nice to catch up on sleeping. That idea was out the window.

She dressed as quickly as possible, while instructing Martin to warm up the car. One look at her boyfriend's face informed he was not sober enough to drive. She felt like crying.

Her father was also incapacitated. She seriously considered going alone, but she knew he would never forgive her. She tried to focus on restraint as she calmly asked both men to gear up as quickly as possible.

Martin said nothing, his police intuition telling him something was wrong. He fought against the effects of the alcohol, straining to force himself to remember his training. He assisted Jenna as best he could in dressing her father.

Against Thomas Coyne's protests, they left the fire going. The young doctor's tone had implied that time was at a premium, and they would have to forego safety and trust no embers would leap out.

The next hour of her life was like a dream. Jenna's worst fear came true. She had suspected as much. Her mother had already passed, maybe even while she was chatting with Vicky.

The explanations were weird and varied, cancer, heart failure, staph infection, she thought all were mentioned in the debriefing. Jenna said nothing, nodding, but not listening to the hospital staff. She could only focus her shame and humiliation while staring at the two most important men in her life, both drunk and uncomprehending.

She walked past both of them and into the restroom, where she could have a cry.

Mother Nature added to the torment by dumping another half foot of snow in the next couple of days as Jenna prepared for her mother's funeral. The wake was barely attended. The Coynes were elderly and had few friends. All of Jenna's friends were either away or unable to venture up North due to the snowfall.

She hadn't even bothered to call the Ruiz women. Why ruin their vacation? The Espositos had sent flowers as well as Grant Maxwell. Vicky and Kyle offered their services, but Jenna had graciously declined.

She didn't want the company, nor the sympathy. She had relegated herself to the role of caretaker, her father unable to handle the funeral preparations.

Martin wisely stood in the shadows, sheepishly ashamed of his prior actions. He had profusely apologized, but Jenna had shrugged off his advances. She acknowledged his alcoholism, and oddly enough, she was indifferent.

Maybe he was beyond redemption? Maybe this was his natural course?

Either way, she had to put the situation on the back burner and deal with the immediate issue.

When the final visitor departed the funeral parlor, Jenna thanked the undertaker and agreed upon the designated time for the funeral. The man had been pleasant enough, sensing the cold distance between Jenna, her father, and her boyfriend.

Her mother had been adamant upon cremation, which suited Jenna just fine. With the havoc that the early winter was whipping at them, an outdoor burial would have been difficult. As it stood currently, getting back to the funeral parlor would be treacherous.

Jenna welcomed the stormy weather. It forced her mind to concentrate on travel, rather than her sorrow. She had grown cold to Martin since leaving the bathroom at her mother's hospital. There was a time when she would have clung to the giant officer, but no longer.

Her ordeal last summer had prepared her for this moment. She was no longer the little girl who relied on daddy, and she sure as all hell wasn't going to transfer that responsibility to any other man. No, she had learned that control was the answer. She had become a decision maker. She smiled recalling one of Grant Maxwell's poetic suggestions when encountering a problem.

Shit or get off the pot, kid!

She had slept well that night. Exhaustion had taken over, and only the sound of the alarm clock had woken her. Both Martin and Thomas Coyne had already risen and were dressed to go. She could sense their guilt, yet glided past them as if nothing had happened.

She maintained that attitude through the services, right up to the presentation of her mother's condolence book. Her blank expression never wavered, even after her father promptly poured a drink upon entering the home. She simply kissed him on the forehead and told him she loved him.

Martin didn't accept an offer of imbibing. Instead, he stood clumsily rubbing at his bad arm. Jenna strutted over and hugged him and also whispered her love. She then retreated to her childhood bedroom, condolence book tucked under her arms.

She flipped through the pages casually. Only a few were written on. Maybe twenty or so people had attended the wake. She scanned through the scribbled signatures until her finger halted to a screech upon the second page. There it was in perfect cursive handwriting.

Lilith Hannigan

Jenna felt her fingers numb up. She fought to grip the book, but it had already tumbled from her unresponsive hands. In slow motion, she watched it fall to the floor, before she slowly sunk down after it.

"You can't remember this lady?" Vicky asked. Her expression suggested disbelief.

"It's driving me crazy," answered Jenna.

A week had passed since her mother's funeral. She had decided to stay in Salem with Vicky for a time. Jenna implied that her girlfriend would need the help getting acclimated to the new job. Not surprisingly, Martin Conrad hadn't protested the decision.

The two women were returning home from the Haverhill office of Esposito Insurance Agency on the commuter rail, happy to be inside a warm train while the cold weather continued to ravage New England.

"Didn't you say only a handful of people showed at the services?"

Jenna nodded. "Yes, that's what is killing me. I would have noticed a middle aged woman. All of my mom's friends were elderly."

"Maybe it was a cruel joke someone played?"

"I don't know, Vicky. Martin and I haven't brought up the subject with anyone else." She ran a hand over her face. "No, it must have been her!"

Vicky remained quiet while the conductor punched their tickets, but then she spoke. "I'm really sorry what happened between you and Sarge. I wish I could have been there to comfort you."

"Forget it. The roads were too dangerous, and besides, Mister Esposito needed your help. How has he been treating you?"

With the mention of their employer, Vicky perked up. "Bill is fantastic. He took care of all the paper work, and he sets up everything for Kyle. Plus, he's a gentleman."

Jenna giggled. "Bill is it? Don't get too comfy around that old charmer. He's got the eye for pretty young girls."

"No, not at all. It's just Kyle is such a baby, with his video games and comics. It's refreshing to talk to a grown-up. Besides, once you returned, I became invisible."

"He does let his eyes linger. "

Vicky smiled and touched Jenna's knee lightly. "Anyway, what about the big guy. Are you going to go home to him?"

Jenna feigned anger. "Trying to get rid of me already?"

"No, it's just..."

"Relax, Vicky. I'm planning on giving Martin sometime to work out his issues. He may be an alcoholic, but that's a label people are quick to throw out. I just feel he needs to get back to work."

Vicky nodded, unsure how to reply.

"Besides, I like taking the train home with you. With Marta gone, I was going stir crazy for company."

"When are her and her mother returning?"

"This weekend. I know Edna will be furious I didn't tell her about Mom, but I couldn't ruin their vacation. Marta was looking forward to it so much."

Vicky sighed. "Marta's okay, but her mom is one tough cookie. She has never forgiven me for last summer."

"You're right about her being tough." Jenna recalled Edna wielding a baseball bat while chasing off her attackers. "Give it time and you'll see how much fun she is."

"I'm sure, Jen. You were right about Bill, and Kyle and I will always remember what you and Sarge did for us." She grabbed Jenna's hand. "What you still are doing for us."

Jenna returned the squeeze, grateful for the distraction her friend had provided in her time of consternation.

Her thoughts were interrupted by the announcement of their station arrival.

Martin Conrad was sure the home was empty. He had debated his move for days, until a surge of alcohol fueled courage forced his hand. He had waited outside the Hannigan house for three hours, idling his car at the base of the street. He had pulled up with the headlights turned off.

Convinced no one was home, he glided across the lawn, a stealth figure dressed in black. The back door proved no obstacle for the disabled lawman. He entered as quietly as possible, keeping the flashlight handy but off.

It was Friday night. His internet research had told him David Hannigan would be at one of the biker clubs, probably in distant Exeter. He knew the man lived alone.

A search of the first floor turned up nothing. The home was shockingly clean, filled with modern furnishings. Martin had expected the opposite. Even the refrigerator revealed no sign of beer or excess.

The bedroom also proved fruitless. The sheets were unmade, but little else attracted notice. The closet and dressers were filled with jeans and t-shirts. Again, nothing to shed light on.

Martin's trained police eye noticed the lack of photos in the home. He didn't know how unusual this was. The man had no spouse and apparently was in some type of feud with his sister whom he claimed to be married to another woman.

Just as he opened the cellar door, Martin felt a shiver tingle down his spine, but he was a second too late in trying to close it. His flashlight revealed a bared a set of canine teeth before the animal barreled into him. The burly giant toppled over, his mind trying to register what happened.

He lost the grip on his flashlight as he fell to the ground. His last image was that of a pink and white pitbull surging toward him before the darkness took over.

Martin felt teeth clamp on to his dangling left arm. Not surprisingly, he felt no pain. For once the deadened arm had proven useful. He instinctively reached for his service revolver.

"Fuck me."

He had left it in the glove compartment. He had been sober enough to realize the potential problems of breaking and entering with a weapon. He hadn't expected to encounter resistance.

The dog's growling became louder as its jaws locked down on skin and bone.

Martin lifted his left arm and swung it against the wall. The animal grunted but did not release its grip. A slick wetness began to crawl down Martin's arm. He knew it was the dog's foaming drool mixed with the big Irishman's own blood.

He continued to thrash around, banging the mutt against any surface he could find. The darkness left him at a disadvantage as he tripped over the bottom stair. All of the air left his lungs as he landed flat on his back.

A rubber cylinder scraped his hand. He recognized it as the flashlight he had dropped. He clutched it wildly with his good arm and began swinging. The dog whimpered but withstood his ferocious blows.

"Let go you son of a bitch!" he yelled at the animal, but the pitbull was adamant on retaining its grip.

Martin was getting dizzy. Even though he felt no pain, he knew he was losing blood rapidly and with the alcohol in his bloodstream, unconsciousness was inevitable.

"I'm sorry puppy."

He summoned what little energy he had left and began to hammer at the dog's skull with the flashlight. The sickening thuds made him feel guilty, but eventually the dog's teeth unclamped. Although he couldn't see it, Martin knew the animal had lost its bloodlust.

He heard a slight thump as the pitbull keeled over, defeated in its quest for a kill.

Martin barely had time to catch his breath as the cellar lights were turned on. Reflexes kicked in and he looked at his mangled arm. The sleeves of both his coat and sweatshirt had been ripped off. So had most of the flesh. He almost feinted at the sight.

"Motherfucker!"

The voice drifted from the top of the stairway. There stood David Hannigan, back early from his Friday night sojourn.

Martin straightened up, ready for attack.

He was not disappointed.

The sinewy biker rambled down the stairs two at a time and hurled himself at the blood drenched Irishman. The momentum of the lunge carried both men into the wall. Martin took the brunt of the blow. His breath left him as his knees wobbled.

David Hannigan reacted immediately with an overhand right to the big man's jaw. Martin stumbled back, his head again striking the wall. He tried to evade the next blow but was only moderately successful as a fist clipped his ear.

"I'll kill you for what you did to my dog!" The biker vowed.

Martin knew the blood loss and alcohol had severely hampered him. His only chance would be to get in close and keep the fight tight to the vest where he could use his nearly hundred pound weight advantage.

David Hannigan had other ideas.

A trained brawler, he sized up the situation immediately and began to counter Martin's moves. He peppered the big man with shots to his damaged arm while moving to the left each time.

Martin didn't feel the blows, but he was unable to keep up with the fancy footwork. He cursed inwardly as the biker landed a body shot that staggered him to his knees.

"You're finished fucker."

Hannigan looped a fist around the side of Martin's head, catching him below the ear. The force of the blow jarred his teeth loose.

Martin glimpsed a last look at the dead canine before his eyes rolled up and his world went dark.

Martin Conrad awoke, wishing he were dead. His skull throbbed madly. He wasn't sure what was worse, the dull ache from the battle or skull-creasing hangover he was suffering from.

It was still dark, and a brief moment of panic ensued.

I'm blind!

The hulking officer reached for his eyes instinctively, but discovered his hands were bound behind his back with handcuffs. He also realized he was on his stomach laying flat. He was locked in some type of enclosure.

A moment later it dawned on him that he had been locked inside the trunk of a car. His suspicion was confirmed when the latch popped open.

David Hannigan's face appeared in the moonlight. The biker snarled menacingly.

"Glad you're still alive, you fat fuck."

He thrust a chop at Martin's exposed neck, choking him.

"I'd finish you myself, but I have to get my dog to a vet. She's a tough little shit. "

Martin's eyes began to adjust to their surroundings. The interior of the car trunk looked familiar. He recognized some of his old gym clothing.

They locked me in my own car!

David Hannigan turned his gaze sideways as Martin heard the sound of approaching footsteps. He counted two pair.

"Is that the piece of shit that hurt my Eddie?"

It was the neighbor who had battled Jenna and Martin over a parking spot.

"Sure is." The biker answered.

The woman leaned closer. Her breath reeked of marijuana. She was dressed in a grey hoodie and jeans. Even in the pale moonlight, Martin could see her sunken eyelids and coke stretched nostrils.

"You sack of shit!" she cursed. "They had to wire my Eddie's jaw shut. He can't even smoke a cigarette because of you and your whore."

Martin wasn't listening. He was weighing his options.

He knew the handcuffs were his own police issued. They had been in the glove compartment. So had his service revolver.

These bastards have my gun!

David Hannigan grinned. "You're in good hands now. I even patched up your arm so you'd last a little longer. I just wish I could have cut you up and fed you to Lucy. That's my dog. The dog you hammered into the ground when you broke into my home." He spit a wad of phlegm on Martin's forehead. "I don't know what your game is, but it's over."

The beefy biker lifted his shirt and removed a weapon. Martin recognized the handle of his gun instantly. It sent shivers down his spine.

"You don't have to do…" he never finished the sentence. David Hannigan reached over and pounded a fist into his neck, slamming the big man's head against the floorboard.

Martin groaned and slipped into unconsciousness.

"You okay with this?" the biker inquired.

The woman nodded enthusiastically. "Oh yeah. " She waved to the driver in the car parked in front of Martin's, presumably her husband Eddie.

David Hannigan handed her the revolver. "Be careful. Drive him far away from Manchester and make sure no one hears the shot. Use some of those old gym clothes to muffle the noise."

The woman continued to nod. She reached an ungloved hand to Hannigan's crotch and stroked him.

"What's that about?" he asked.

She kissed him hard on the lips. "Because when we get back, I'm going to give you the best blowjob you've ever had! Eddie won't mind. Fuck, he'll be getting off on this for weeks."

Hannigan returned her kiss and slapped her behind. "Remember, not around here!" He took one last look at Martin Conrad's unconscious form. "Don't shoot him in the head. Make the fucker bleed out. Lucy would appreciate it."

"You bet."

The woman slammed the trunk hard. She blew a kiss in the direction of her husband before stepping into the driver's seat of Martin's car. David Hannigan watched them depart.

"Adios, fucker!"

Martin's eyes stung. The exhaust fumes were gagging him. Only the relief of the frosty air seeping into the trunk kept him from choking on his own vomit.

His head felt like a hornet's nest.

He had no idea how long he was out. It must have been awhile. His body was sore and his arms were numb from being prone.

He tried to remain calm and survey his surroundings. The car was traveling fast. In these icy conditions that meant they were on the highway. He heard no other noise. That told him they were out of the city and heading into rural New Hampshire.

His ears perked as the radio snapped on. He couldn't be sure how many people were in the car, or who was driving. He doubted David Hannigan was present. He recalled his passion fueled speech about Lucy the dog.

Martin was pleased. He didn't think he could survive another encounter with the biker, not in his present condition anyway.

The odor of reefer began to drift into the back. The driver had lit up.

Must be that ugly hag!

He remembered her stench from earlier. He also remembered what he had done to her husband, Eddie.

Self-defense for sure, but try explaining that to his old lady.

After a few more minutes, the radio was turned off and he felt the car

His head felt like a hornet's nest.

began to slow and make a turn into a lot.

This is it. Killed with my own weapon!

The car came to an abrupt halt and then the engine ceased. The driver got out and then it became silent.

More time passed and then the trunk latch popped open.

A leering face peeked in.

Eddie!

"My husband would greet you but he can't talk. In fact, he will never talk well again. You made him bite the tip of his tongue off!"

Eddie remained emotionless. His eyes were vacant, contemplating. He withdrew the service revolver and cupped it cautiously.

Martin's throat was dry. He choked briefly before uttering a few words.

"I need you to think this through. I am a Boston police officer. I will be missed. They will find out what happened, and they will pursue you. You have one chance..."

Eddie slammed the butt of the gun down on his forehead. Blood gashed from Martin's scalp.

"Not so fast, Eddie!" his wife pleaded. "Davey, said to make this prick suffer. Maybe we should shoot his balls off?"

Martin remained calm, hoping to reason.

"They know I was at his house. They will put two and two together and figure it out."

"Shut up!" She slapped him hard, her bare hand stinging his lips. She stood back and glared at Martin. "What the hell were you doing in Davey's home?"

Martin drew in a breath of the chilly air. He tried to shake off the buzzing inside his skull.

"Well?" She prompted again.

The burly officer decided on telling it straight.

"My girlfriend, she..."

"The blonde slut that helped you hurt my Eddie?"

He ignored her commentary. "David's sister, Lilith, might be her mother."

The woman laughed. Eddie tried to echo the sentiment. He couldn't open his jaw, so it looked like he was suffering some sort of convulsion.

"That old butch. She's a rug muncher. No way she spread her legs for the pole."

Martin continued, secretly stalling for some hope of an intervention.

"Twenty-five years ago, Lilith Hannigan was involved in a transaction that resulted in the purchase of a baby girl by a young couple in Franklin."

Eddie shivered and wrapped his arms around himself, indicating he was cold.

Martin ignored him.

"We have reason to believe David might have been involved."

The woman ignored Marty and hugged her husband.

"I guess it ain't gonna hurt to talk to you, seeing my Eddie is going to stick that gun up your ass and fire it."

Martin gulped, he knew she was serious.

The woman continued. "Davey use to make some side money selling photos of kids back in the day."

Martin closed his eyes in disgust.

"It weren't so bad. Just kiddie pics, no sex or anything. Sides, the young ones don't remember. Hell, me and Eddie let him take a few of my boys. That's how we paid for that house."

Martin gritted his teeth in anger. "How did his sister fit into this?"

"She supplied most of the children. Either through baby-sitting or later on at a daycare, she would do all the regular stuff. You know feeding the little shits, changing diapers and all. Davey would take Polaroids and sell them. They didn't have no internet back then."

Eddie was getting restless. He dropped an elbow on Martin's temple. Pain roared though the big Irishman, but he remained awake.

"My husband's getting tired. They got him so pumped up on pain killers, he falls asleep half the day. Not that the fucker was all that energetic to begin with. I'm surprised he didn't fuck up our car on the way here."

Martin saw an opening. "Where are we?"

"Just past Rumney, inside the Polar Caves. Ain't no one here after labor day and they sure as all hell won't hear gunshots around these parts."

Polar Caves.

Martin remembered visiting them several times during his youth. The roadside attraction was off the beaten path. She was correct. No one would be around. Not during the winter, not during this weather.

"You can still walk away from this," he stated.

The woman turned toward her husband. He still revealed the same stoic face he had displayed earlier.

"No can do. You know us and we can't cross Davey."

Martin tried to think of something. Before a thought could surface, Eddie moved forward and jammed the gun against his chest.

"Please, I…"

Eddie didn't let him finish. He pulled the trigger twice. The revolver flared, lighting up the parking lot, as the slugs slammed into Martin Conrad's chest.

The big Irishman grunted. His lips formed a word before his world turned black.

Jenna....

«—»

"Something is wrong!"

Jenna Coyne bolted into the bedroom of Vicky Robinson's modest Salem home.

"What? Huh?" Vicky responded, yanking out her earplugs. She had been quietly dozing, having given up on Kyle coming to bed an hour ago. She cast a glance at the digital clock on her nightstand. It proclaimed the time to be shortly after midnight.

Vicky yanked back the covers. She was wearing gray sweats and a cutoff t-shirt. It barely covered her stomach scars, souvenirs courtesy of her father's drunken sprees. The late John Robinson had gotten off on burning his daughter with cigarettes, a claim he adamantly denied.

"Calm down and climb in," she ordered.

Jenna obeyed, slipping her trembling body under the warm blankets.

"I'm sorry, Vicky," she started. "I had the weirdest feeling that something happened to Marty."

"What are you talking about?" Vicky asked gently.

"I can't explain. I was awake, reading, when I got to wondering what Martin was up to. I know it's late, but he isn't answering the phone."

Vicky snorted with amusement. "Jenna, honey. He's a big boy. He probably drank a few too many and passed out."

Jenna shook her head in defiance. "No, he's never gone to bed without talking to me, not even before I moved in with him."

"I'm sure it's nothing. All this shoveling probably wore him out." Vicky flipped over and turned off the light. "It's late, just lay here with me and we'll call him in the morning."

"Are you sure?" Jenna asked. "I mean, what about Kyle? Where will he sleep?"

Vicky waved a hand nonchalantly. "Forget about him. It took me awhile, but I figured out Kyle is just one big infant. He'll stay in the den playing videogames and smoking weed until he gets tired, and then when he does come to bed, he starts snoring before his head hits the pillow. I can't remember the last time he touched me." She didn't wait for Jenna to say anything. "Truthfully, ever since I sobered up I realized Kyle is nothing more than a roommate."

"Sorry," Jenna mumbled.

"Don't be. I needed my eyes opened. I just didn't know better. Kyle seemed like a better alternative than my daddy, but that's only because I didn't really know any real men, like Marty or Billy."

"There you go with that Billy thing again."

Vicky frowned. "I know you had some problems with Bill in the past, but I have to admit he is a wonderful guy."

Jenna felt her stomach churn. "He's creepy, with the fake toupee and the outdated wardrobe. It's all so cheesy."

"What's wrong with a man who cares about his appearance? Christ, Kyle thinks washing his balls and armpits is his idea of a shower. I think it's great that Bill takes pride in himself. Besides, if you feel that way about him, why do you stay? You could get another job."

Jenna was dumbfounded. She couldn't reply to the question. It dawned on her that she had conquered so many obstacles in her life recently that a career switch should seem like a no brainer. Her sour mood turned bright.

"You are one hundred percent correct, Vicky. I am free to look elsewhere."

Vicky draped an arm over her friend. "I'm sorry I opened my big mouth. I enjoy your company at the office. Anyway, forget about Bill, and let Martin have his space for now. We need to get some sleep."

Jenna flipped over, but was unable to close her eyes. For the first night since she had met him, Martin Conrad hadn't wished her a goodnight.

Jenna struggled with the steering wheel, unfamiliar with the motor vehicle. She had convinced Bill Esposito to loan her one of his "beaters" that he kept on-hand for customers to use while their own automobiles were being repaired. Unlike, rental agencies which carried a fleet of swift new models, Esposito Insurance, sported questionable vehicles, that lacked reliability.

Vicky Robinson had promised to cover her office shift again today, a little too enthusiastically. Jenna wondered what spell her flirting employer had cast on her naive friend. Vicky appeared to be smitten by the snake charmer.

Jenna's thoughts were disrupted by the roaring horn of an eighteen wheeler. She had mistakenly drifted over the median line on 93 North heading to New Hampshire. The blaring noise startled her.

"Christ!" she cursed.

Against all advice, she had decided to venture out looking for Martin Conrad. Despite the fact that she had known him only for a brief time, she had formed a potent bond with the rugged Boston police officer. She had no doubt in her mind that the big lug had ventured back to Manchester to pursue Jenna's identity quest.

The treacherous roads challenged her young driving skills like never before. There were few vehicles out on the highway, but she dared not travel faster than ordinary.

"You had better be okay, Marty," she whispered aloud.

The snow continued to fall haphazardly as she concentrated on her effort. Fortunately, the trip didn't involve much navigation. She would stay on the main highway through Massachusetts and deep into New Hampshire.

Her cell-phone chimed.

"Marty?" she blurted into the phone.

"No, sorry," a familiar voice answered. "It's me, Vicky."

Jenna hid her disappointment. "Did Martin call the office?"

"No, Jenna. Bill and I have been here all day. It's too cold to go outside. Martin hasn't called here."

Jenna groaned. "Okay, I probably shouldn't tie up my line, in case he rings."

"Hold on Jenna, Bill, ..er, Mr. Esposito wants to talk to you." She passed the phone over to her amorous employer.

"Jenna?" the voice inquired.

Jenna recognized Bill Esposito's squeaky tone. "Yes, sir?"

The middle aged man cleared his throat, as if he were going to make an announcement. "Jenna, I did some more digging on Lilith Hannigan."

Jenna had allowed her mind to put her search for Hannigan on the back burner as she focused on her mother's death and Martin's disappearance.

"What did you learn?" she asked.

"I was able to track her Continental back to the original dealership. The owner is an old friend of mine, and he is old school, keeps ledgers, photo copies, the works."

Jenna could hear the excitement in Esposito's breath. He was like a little kid bringing his report card home to his parents.

"Please, Bill," Jenna begged. "I don't want to tie the line up in case Martin calls. Can you just tell me what you know?"

Esposito snorted with a hint of contempt, but then he let out a sigh. "Of course, Jenna, no problem. Martin should be the issue here."

"But?" she prompted.

"Well the old geezer still had the vin number in his files, and he matched it with his records. The car was sold to Lilith Hannigan, but the down payment check was written out by someone else."

Jenna was losing her mind. "Bill, please, stop with the dramatics. Who wrote the check?"

Once again, she could almost feel the little man's bubble deflating. "Thomas Coyne." he answered meekly.

"My dad?" Jenna wondered. "He bought that Lincoln?"

"Probably, at the least he put down a hefty two thousand dollar deposit. I hope that news helps you Jenna."

Numb, all Jenna could do was thank her boss, and hang up on him. She was already over the border, and the snow appeared to be thickening. If she could just hold out for another half hour, she would be in downtown Manchester.

Jenna Coyne parked the loaner a street over from the Hannigan house. The last thing she wanted was another confrontation with stickman Eddie and his vulgar wife. Confident the pair were not lurking about, the desperate sleuth forced herself to inch closer to the biker's Manchester house.

The mediocre home was dark, not a single light shining. Jenna prayed the homeowner was absent, hopefully knocking back cheap beer at one of the downtown taverns. The novice trespasser considered trying the front door, but thought better of it. Even if no one were home, it was possible surveillance cameras might betray her criminal act.

Pulling her ski cap down over her blonde hair, she tiptoed around to the back of the house, expecting to be attacked by a guard dog or even worse, a wild animal, but it, too, was lifeless. She let out a breath of air, and soaked in the situation.

The lights were out. There were no signs of animals. It was freezing outside.

Without hesitation, Jenna reached down and plucked up an ice laden rock and violently smashed the exposed glass panel on the rear door. The cracking of the glass echoed a hundred times louder than it should have, but still, not a stir from within nor outside the house. Deftly, she slid a slender hand around the shards of glass and unlocked the door. She swung it open and counted to five before dashing inside.

Again, the silence was deafening. Jenna was sure the neighbors must have heard something, but then she let reasoning take over. The snow was still falling, and the fierce New Hampshire winds were howling. Not even a brave soul would have ventured out to investigate.

Smug in her satisfaction, she snatched her cell phone from her ski jacket and turned on the flashlight feature. It shone just bright enough for her to see in the dark, but surely not enough beam to be spotted from the outside.

She allowed her eyes to scan the room and soak in the layout. Surprisingly, the house was tidy. She had expected the stereo typical biker pad, decked out with empty liquor bottles, remnants of marijuana and porn everywhere. Instead, she saw a rather boring kitchen that looked like a magazine photo shoot. The only hint of occupation were a few photos of David Hannigan and his friends stuck to the refrigerator with magnets.

Determined to locate Martin Conrad, the plucky sleuth ventured out of the kitchen and into a small hallway where she saw a door open. It led to the basement she guessed. A shudder went down Jenna's spine as she descended the stairway. After three steps, she did an about face, and sprinted back up to the top, her nerves finally getting the better of her.

Turned out her instincts were correct. Her paranoia became reality as she heard an angry bellow come from the kitchen doorway.

"What the hell?" cursed an angry David Hannigan upon noticing his home had been broken into.

Jenna froze. She tried to force her body to move, but she was paralyzed. The biker's gruff voice had startled her, and she was unable to react. She cursed her weakness.

"Whoever the fuck you are, you're dead!" Hannigan promised as he spotted the open cellar door.

Despite the warning, Jenna remained immobile, trying to summon up her courage. Her months of training were supposed to have prepared her for this moment, but her mind was twisted in confusion and panic.

Before she could do or say anything, David Hannigan was upon her. With a maniacal growl, he lunged his frame at her.

The impact was brutal. Jenna was driven into the sheet rocked wall, the back of head denting it and causing her to see stars. As the breath flew from her lungs, Jenna felt the biker's corded muscles wrap around her shoulders.

"Bitch!" he raged, tossing her down the remaining stairs.

Jenna felt herself take flight, unable to maintain her footing. She sailed through the air, landing harshly on her hip. She yelped helplessly as she struggled to get up.

Hannigan did not hesitate. Hurtling himself down the stairs two at a time, he landed a crushing knee into Jenna's backside. Tremendous pain overwhelmed the young woman as she desperately tried to assess her situation.

She tried to recollect her self defense courses, fleeting images and memories flooding her mind, but the biker's actions were too fast to allow her thoughts to register. Before she could muster up any type of defense, he was raining blows upon her.

Jenna reeled from the relentless attack. She felt like a rag doll under the brutal assault. This was nothing like her trainer had exposed her to. These punches were real and vicious. She felt blood dripping from her chin.

"You little bitch!" Hannigan snarled. "First, your tub of lard boyfriend comes here and hurts my boy, and now you show up. I'll kill you!"

Jenna ignored his threat. Her mind narrowed on his comments regarding Martin Conrad. So, the rugged police office had returned to Manchester and apparently had come to this very same house.

"Where is he?" Jenna croaked. "Where's Martin?"

Hannigan ceased his attack, amused by her questioning. "Seriously? You're asking about that fat blob? Do you have any idea what I'm going to do to you?"

Jenna swallowed a mouthful of her own blood and repeated her request. "Where is he?" The lean biker tilted his head back and let out a devilish laugh. He licked the blood from his knuckles as he leered at Jenna. She shuddered at his lusty gaze.

"I'm afraid you will be needing to find a new man, sweet cheeks. That big buffalo is permanently out of commission."

Jenna felt as if a knife had been twisted in her gut. The pain and terror was far worse than the physical blows the biker had inflicted.

"Martin…" she moaned.

"Was that his name?" Hannigan mocked. "Martin? Marty?" He yanked her ski cap off, revealing her disheveled hair. "My, my, I can see why Tubbo took a liking to you." He yanked her hair violently, pulling her body closer. He sniffed wildly at her mane.

Jenna struggled to break his grip, but he was too strong for her. She felt helpless, even more so than her deadly battle in her North End apartment many months ago. She had rallied to survive that epic encounter, but this outcome didn't appear as promising.

"Tell me, blondie, before I kill you, and rest assured, I will kill you, why are you here? What the hell are you and your boyfriend looking for?"

Jenna began to sob. She was ashamed of herself, but the realization that Martin Conrad was dead, had been the final straw. Defeated, she could no longer summon the energy to go on.

Angered by her hesitation, David Hannigan tightened his grip upon her hair. With a might heave, he lifted her tiny frame from the ground by the roots of her hair.

Jenna screamed in agony. Her mind ordered her to fight back. Visions of kicking and biting flicked in and out of her mind, but she was unable to muster up the physical action required to inflict any damage.

Hannigan was overjoyed by her helplessness. He pushed a cabled arm forward, heaving her down to the floor again. She lay there in the fetal position, her body begging for relief. The biker took the time to jog up the stairs, and close the door. He flicked on the light switch.

Jenna looked down and saw she had landed in a pool of blood. Her eyes widened madly, as she clawed at the sticky floor.

"Martin!" she gasped in horror.

"Oh no!" Hannigan informed her. "I suppose some of it might be that piece of shit's blood, but what you're swimming in honey is what that fat son of bitch did to my dog. Right now he's at the vet fighting for his life, but rest assured he will not die in vain. No, that little bugger was one tough son of a bitch. Gave your boyfriend a battle, for sure."

Jenna tried to calm her sobbing. "Please, Martin, where is he?"

Hannigan was amused. "Probably inside the belly of a hungry wolf by now. Come to think of it, that boy had a lot of meat on his bones, probably enough to feed the pack."

Jenna forced herself to stop sobbing. Her face was beginning to swell from the punches he had landed, and her head was throbbing from pain. She managed to get up on all fours.

Hannigan let out a wolf whistle. "Don't you worry mama. I'm going to get to that before you leave this heavenly world. In fact, right there in that bloody patch your sliding in."

Jenna recoiled at his threat. This only amused Hannigan even more. He licked his lips like a madman. "Before I stick it in you, I want you to answer my question. I asked you why you were here."

"Martin," was all Jenna could reply.

"Yeah, yeah, yeah. Bean bag Marty. Don't make me mess you up more, girl."

Jenna regained her composure. Her teeth felt loose. She wondered if they would fall out.

"Last chance," Hannigan threatened.

The brave girl nodded in understanding. She muttered one word. "Lilith."

"Lilith?" Hannigan parroted. "My dyke sister? This is about her? What happened? The old coot going for young trim now? You and fat boy into some kinky shit?"

Jenna repeated herself. "Lilith."

Frustrated, Hannigan planted his booted foot into her midsection, knocking the air from Jenna's lungs.

"I warned you bitch!" He snapped, slapping her harshly across the face. "You had your chance."

Jenna shielded herself with a limp arm, her body trembling. "Lilith." she began, "She…Lincoln Continental…pizza."

Hannigan stifled his attack, aware the girl was losing comprehension.

"What about my sister? Yeah she had a Lincoln."

Jenna seemed to be in a trance. She was listing off words in a weird utterance. It was clear, she had suffered a breakdown.

"The children…pizza."

Hannigan stiffened up. His features froze in a deathly complexion. "Listen, that was a longtime ago. We were kids making a few bucks selling photos to diddlers. We never let them touch those kids."

"Pizza…the photo," Jenna muttered.

"Wait a minute!" Hannigan paused. "You're one of them! You're one of the little bastards we photographed." He looked at her in appraisal. "Looks like you turned out okay."

Jenna didn't answer, she just began to rock back and forth catatonically. "Lincoln."

"Freed the slaves," Hannigan finished, amusing herself. "Listen Blondie, I gotta move things along. You can keep the jacket on, but lose the jeans."

Jenna remained motionless.

"Now," the angry biker snapped.

No response at all. Jenna had snapped her mind unable to comprehend the dire situation.

Undeterred, David Hannigan lurched forward, intent on satisfying his carnal urge. He tore at her waist, determined to have his way with her. Jenna continued to rock back and forth, her mind having freed itself from the horror.

Hannigan was tearing at her jeans, trying to rip them from her frail body, when he heard a primal growl from the top of the stairway. A massive silhouette framed the doorway, its shadow projected on the wall monstrously.

Before the shocked biker could react, the intruder had hurled himself down the stairway, cannonball style. His massive frame landed sickening on the powerful biker, but even David Hannigan's well chiseled body could not endure the aerial attack. He was driven past Jenna and crushed violently against the blood riddled concrete floor.

Jenna, herself, did not react to the carnage. She continued to rock back and forth as the battle raged on. David Hannigan tried to resume his stance, but was met with a torrid of rage as his aggressor continued to pummel him.

The shadowy figure was not to be halted in his conquest. He lashed out at the startled biker, knocking him out cold, upon the blood swept floor. Even then, the attacker continued the assault, violently battering the unconscious form. He was about to strike a deathblow with his knee to Hannigan's neck when a meek voice startled him out of his killer rage.

"Martin!" Jenna gasped, escaping her trance.

The rugged cop, turned, his face momentarily frozen in homicidal rage. He appeared driven to strike a fatal blow anyway, but at the last second forced himself to cease. Instead, he kicked the knocked out biker in the testicles.

"Martin?" Jenna muttered again, this time making eye contact.

The faithful police officer lifted her to her feet. She struggled with her tattered clothes, unaware how close she had been to being violated by David Hannigan.

"Everything will be okay, Jenna," the police man confided.

She stared up at her savior's face. Like her, he too, had suffered a great deal of physical punishment this evening. She stared at his chest. He was wearing a police issued bullet proof vest. She could see holes in the fabric.

"Martin? What happened?"

The burly Townie, grinned. "Long story, baby. Right now, I'd better call my new best friends at the Manchester PD. Seems like we have quite a story to tell."

She cut him off before he could say anything else, wrapping her arms around the big man. She saw his wounded arm was bleeding profusely from teeth wounds.

"Oh my God, Marty!"

Martin Conrad shrugged. "Don't worry, I can't feel it at all. Finally, my useless arm served a purpose." He pulled handcuffs from his back pocket. "Remind me to tell you about these bad boys some day."

Jenna Coyne hugged him fiercely.

Martin Conrad was treated for possible rabies infection and extreme blood loss. His bullet proof vest had saved his life, but still left him with severe bruising. His chest was a deep purplish color that was sore to the touch.

The rugged Boston Police officer would spend a long time explaining his actions to his superiors. The breaking and entering might be forgiven, but getting shot with his own weapon was unforgivable. He knew his career in law enforcement had come to an end. He decided to keep this information away from the brooding Jenna Coyne.

Jenna, too, had been treated by medical personnel. David Hannigan had inflicted a tremendous beating upon her body. Fortunately, she hadn't lost any teeth, but her face was bloated and discolored. He had broken her nose and blackened both eyes. She was ashamed to let Martin Conrad see her in this condition, but the big man had insisted.

"Martin, all that work I put in, all that training and I just stood there and let him pummel me," she confessed.

Conrad, himself, didn't fare much better. His facial features were a bit out of whack, and he could only guess was his tattered arm looked like. The doctors told him the prognosis for recovery looked dim, but he didn't care. The arm hadn't worked well since the incident in the North End. Amputation seemed inevitable, yet Martin felt a sense of relief.

"Jenna, you can't punish yourself about this. You were taken by surprise by an attacker with a huge advantage over you. There is no shame in being the victim. This isn't your fault."

Jenna shook her head in argument. "That sounded like a pamphlet you must have memorized at the police academy."

Martin reached over and kissed her on the forehead. She was lying prone in a hospital bed, patiently waiting to be discharged.

"All that matters is that you're safe now. He can't hurt you anymore."

The wounded girl let out a long breath of air. She looked at Martin's bandaged arm. "Deja vu?"

The burly officer laughed. "Right? But this time, I did save you. The press won't have to make up a story."

He went on to explain that after he had been shot in the chest and left for dead at the deserted Polar Caves, a stroke of luck had intervened to save his life. A couple of horny students from nearby Plymouth State College had driven to the parking lot for privacy and came across the wounded Boston Police officer. He shuddered to think what might have happened to Jenna if those spunky kids had kept driving.

"What happens now?" Jenna asked timidly.

Martin shrugged. "Depends on the justice system. Hannigan and his neighbors will be charged with attempted murder, but I'm going to have to pay the price for using my authority improperly."

A single tear rolled from Jenna's swollen eye.

"I'm sorry Martin. I know your career meant everything to you, you following in your dad's footsteps, and all."

He gnawed on his lower lip. "I'd do it all over again in a heart beat before allowing anyone to hurt you."

Jenna smiled despite the pain she was experiencing. "You know, in all the excitement, I never found out about my real birth mother, and you know what? I'm okay with that. I had parents growing up, and they were good people. My mom spent her life looking after me, and I appreciate it."

"Me, too, for what it counts." Martin chimed in. "The Coynes raised a special woman. I've been a real jerk these last few months Jenna, and I'm sorry."

She put a finger on his lips.

"No, please." he continued. "I can't imagine life without you, Jenna."

"You won't have to you big lug. Besides, someone will have to change those bandages for you."

THE END

About Our Creators

WRITER

ROBERT RICCI – graduated from of Curry College, class of 1986 and is a lifelong resident of New England who grew up on a steady diet of Doc Savage novels, classic comic strips like Terry and the Pirates, etc. He loves the classic heroes, Flash Gordon, Tarzan, Conan and all the rest. He's also a huge fan of 1960s television series. Last but not least, he's the proud father of two adult young ladies and lives a quiet life with his better half, Dorothy.

INTERIOR ILLUSTRATOR

JASON WREN - is an American born artist and designer residing in Auburn, Alabama. In 2000, Jason received his BFA from the University of Montevallo with a concentration in painting. Since that time, he has pursued art as both a passion and a career. Much of his early work consists of classically inspired portraits and children's book illustrations. From the years 2010 to 2017, Jason lived in Finland where he worked as an illustrator, designer and teacher. His commissioned works from that time can be found across Scandinavia, England and New Zealand. Upon returning to the US in 2017, Jason and his family settled in Alabama where he continues to follow the path of creativity.

COVER ARTIST

TED HAMMOND - is a Canadian artist who has been creating amazing art for over twenty years. His work has appeared in magazines, ads, books and graphic novels just to name a few. Go to (www.tedhammond.com) to contact him and check out more of his work!

Printed in Great Britain
by Amazon

37567779R00089